"I had my physician call the ER doctor and afterward, when we discussed their conversation, he suggested that I get her to a specialist as quickly as possible."

"A specialist at Boston Children's," Richard said with a nod. "What kind of specialist?"

"A pediatric oncologist."

Before Richard could say another word, Jenny's grandmother spoke. "A cancer specialist," Marian said, her voice catching. "They believe Jenny has leukemia."

ONE LAST WISH

Lurlene McDaniel

The Legacy: Making Wishes Come True

Published by
Dell Laurel-Leaf
an imprint of
Random House Children's Books
a division of Random House, Inc.
New York

Visit us on the Web! www.randomhouse.com/teens

Educators and librarians, for a variety of teaching tools, visit us at
www.randomhouse.com/teachers

ISBN: 0-553-56134-0

RL: 5, ages 10 and up

Printed in the United States of America

A Bantam Book/April 1993
First Dell Laurel-Leaf Edition June 2003

20 19 18

OPM

The Legacy:
Making Wishes
Come True

Dear Richard,

As you must know, I too am deeply grieved over the recent death of your father. To the world, he was Richard Holloway II, Esquire, the attorney who so competently handled my legal affairs all these years. For me, he was a faithful and good friend, and I shall miss him greatly. How I regret being too old and ill to come for his funeral.

I'm writing to ask if you will come see me. I need your help to complete an extraordinary project that your father and I started. There's too much to describe in a letter, but I will tell you that it involves our dear Jenny. Since we both have loved her, I felt I could turn to you for help.

I will be at my home in Martha's Vineyard, a place I know you remember well. Please, Richard, come at your earliest convenience. We have much to do, and time is short.

I eagerly await your arrival.
                              Marian Ruth Crawford

RICHARD HOLLOWAY III reread Marian's letter before tucking it into the pocket of his windbreaker and continuing his solitary walk up the windswept strip of deserted beach. He'd met with Marian, and after hearing her plans, he'd come to this place that had been so much a part of his past. He needed somewhere to think about what she'd asked him to do.

"Please help," Marian had pleaded. "We must do this for Jenny."

Overhead, a seagull flung lonely cries against a slate gray sky that threatened rain. *Tears from heaven.* He thought it fitting. Richard skirted the frigid, rolling surf and started toward a soaring cliff of rocks. He was certain he could find the narrow crevice in the wall of granite, even after all these years. His mind churned with thoughts of what Marian had asked of him.

As he climbed up the rocks, memories from that long ago summer bombarded him. He tried to shake them off, but it was impossible. His brain turned time back to the summer of 1978—the summer when Jenny Crawford turned sixteen. He recalled her vividly—black hair blowing in the breeze, sparkling blue eyes the same deep color of the sea. What had she been feeling on that June day she'd met his sailboat at the marina?

One

⌒⌒⌒

JENNY RACED ALONG the dock, her eyes never leaving the taut, white sail that dipped in the stiff wind and dazzling afternoon sunshine. Breathless, she halted at the slip where the *Triple H* would soon dock. She stood on tiptoes, anxiously searching for her first glimpse of Richard behind the sailboat's helm.

She hadn't seen him since the holidays, when he'd come home from Princeton to Boston, spent Christmas Day, then taken off on a yachting trip to the Bahamas. At the time, his brief visit had upset her, but anticipation over his arrival today made her hurt fade.

She thought he looked like a Viking—tall, with wind-whipped golden blond hair shimmering in the sunlight. His skin, bronzed by the sun, made his green eyes glow like jewels. Richard lowered the *Triple H*'s sail and started the motor to maneuver the sailboat quickly into its slip at the dock. "Ahoy!" Richard called, waving.

Jenny's heart beat faster. "Have a good trip over from Hyannis?" she asked as he threw her a line from the bow of the boat.

"Perfect! Nothing like the wind in the sheets and the smell of the sea," he said, jumping from the bow to the dock and tying the line to a post. "I didn't expect a welcoming committee."

He hugged her, and she reveled in his embrace. The moment was over all too quickly. "You didn't? But haven't we always spent our summers together?" She smiled eagerly. "I thought we could go visit our special cave. You know, the way we did when we were kids."

"A nice offer, JC, but I've made other plans for the day."

Jenny's heart sank. "What's so important that you can't sneak away to the cave with me?" She had wanted to surprise him with a picnic basket and a gift she'd stashed inside their secret hideaway.

"Hot date," Richard said.

Jenny felt her stomach tighten. "Who's the lucky girl?"

Richard tossed back his head and laughed. "Hope the girl shares your opinion. She goes to Vassar and is a friend of one of my roommates. He fixed us up."

"Well, don't forget who your old friends are."

"Not a chance." He gave her shoulders a gentle squeeze. "Will you be at the Club Saturday night? I understand Dame Marian has invited my parents to dinner. Dad wants me to come along."

Dame Marian was Richard's pet name for Jenny's grandmother. "Yes, I'll be there. Will you be too busy for me this summer?"

He turned her to face him. "You'll always be my

special girl, and we'll have lots of time to bum around this summer. But right now, I need to smooth things over with my parents."

"What things?"

"My grades came, and Dad blew up. I'm afraid I'm on academic probation."

"That's too bad."

Richard shrugged and stepped back onto the boat as he continued to talk. "It only matters to Dad. He's still set on my going on to law school, even though I've told him a hundred times I don't want to be an attorney and take over the family firm." Richard's duffel bag landed on the dock with a thud. He jumped back over, picked it up, and draped his arm around Jenny's shoulders.

He treats me like a baby sister, she thought with resignation. They walked to the parking lot where Jenny handed over the keys to Richard's Malibu. She'd gone by his house, gotten the keys from his mother, and driven down to the docks. "Thanks," he told her. "Hop in, and I'll drop you off at your place."

Disappointed that they wouldn't be able to spend the afternoon together, she slid across the front seat. She kept thinking about his date and wondered if he would hit it off with this new girl.

"What happened to your legs?" he asked, pointing at large bruises.

She glanced downward and tugged at the hem of her Bermuda shorts. "I don't know. These bruises just started showing up for no reason."

"Some of them look pretty mean." Richard lifted her chin with his forefinger. "You feeling all right?"

She felt as if a train had run over her, but that was

because he was busy with some other girl. "I'm fine."

"You have dark circles under your eyes."

"I didn't sleep very well last night." She almost added, *Because I was thinking of nothing but seeing you.*

He brushed his hand over her cheek. "Maybe you should go for a checkup."

"Good grief. I'm fine. Maybe a little tired, but the last few weeks of school were hectic. Don't mention anything to Grandmother, or she'll have me under lock and key for the summer."

Richard studied her face for a moment, then turned on the ignition, saying, "We couldn't have that, could we? I expect you to save me a dance Saturday night. And don't get any new bruises on those gorgeous legs."

She covered her knees self-consciously and wondered where so many bruises might have come from. Then she put the whole issue out of her mind, because at the moment, she was with Richard. And nothing else in the world was more important to her than that. Nothing.

Richard forced himself to concentrate on driving. It wasn't easy with Jenny sitting so close beside him. He shouldn't have come for the summer. He should have told his parents that he didn't care to make the annual summer trek out to Martha's Vineyard, but his father was angry at him and in no mood for compromise.

"You're quiet," Jenny said. "Thinking about school?"

"I never think about school. That's my problem."

"All right, so you've blown a semester. You can make it up."

"More than the semester. I've blown the whole year."

"You don't sound too remorseful."

Her profile looked cut from fine porcelain, her skin smooth and pale. A little too pale, he thought. "I can't change the past, so why talk about it? How are plans going for your big 'coming out' party?"

"I don't want to be a debutante, but Grandmother's insisting. I can't understand why my introduction to Boston society is so important to her."

"Well you know these Boston bluebloods—they must keep the lineage pure. Can't have a potential carrier such as yourself off mucking up her genes with the riffraff."

Jenny socked him playfully on the arm. "Blueblood! How awful-sounding. It sounds as if my blood's frozen."

"I'm sure Dame Marian wants you to have every opportunity to meet only the most eligible men," Richard said soberly. "That's what coming out parties are all about, you know—so that the finest can officially meet the finest."

Jenny wrinkled her nose. "I want to do something grand with my life. As my father did."

"You want to join the Peace Corps?"

"Perhaps. Would you miss me terribly if I went off to Africa or South America?"

"I'd miss you terribly." He winked, not wanting her to guess how much he would miss her, how much he *did* miss her and had missed her during the past year, when he'd been away at college.

Jenny crossed her arms defiantly. "Honestly, Grandmother treats me like I'm still a child. Doesn't she see how much I've changed? You think I've changed, don't you?"

She had changed all right. He remembered the first time he'd ever seen her. She had been a child of eight, crying at the side of her parents' graves in an old New England cemetery. He had been twelve and had felt sorry for her. Since then, she'd grown from a child into a woman. He thought her beautiful. And very desirable.

He hated himself for the attraction he felt toward her. It wasn't right. They'd practically grown up together. He was twenty. She was sixteen. But he'd been fighting his growing feelings for her for over a year. He'd even gone off on a sailing trip at Christmas trying to keep his mind—and hands—off her.

He couldn't have her—even if there were no age difference. She was a Crawford, the light and life of his father's oldest and most powerful client. He was a nobody, with no purpose and direction for his life, and he certainly didn't have the social background her grandmother wanted for her. "Yes, you've changed," he said, answering her question. "Boston society never had it so good."

"I don't want Boston society," she said stubbornly.

He stopped the car at the gate of Marian Crawford's summer home, and the security guard opened the car door for Jenny. "See you Saturday," he said. He watched her walk away and noticed an enormous red, splotchy bruise on the back of her shapely leg. "You should have those bruises checked out," he called.

"Don't worry about me. Just worry about how you're going to get me to forgive you for running off with some other girl this afternoon."

He started to confess that there was no other girl. That he'd made the whole thing up. It was all a lie, but a necessary lie. He couldn't have her know how he felt about her. "We'll go sailing next week," he said.

She brightened. "Promise?"

He reproached himself for caving in to his desire to be with her. "Promise." He put the car into gear and quickly drove away.

Two

"GOOD MORNING, SLEEPYHEAD. I was beginning to think you weren't going to join me for breakfast. And you know how much I enjoy starting my day with your company," Marian Crawford said as Jenny entered the breakfast room.

Jenny bent and kissed her grandmother's cheek before taking her customary place. The brightness of the morning sun spilling through the windows hurt her eyes. Her whole body ached, and although she'd slept fourteen hours, she felt as if she hadn't slept at all. Her joints hurt, and she felt lightheaded, but she forced herself to ignore her aches and pains. It was Saturday, and she was hours away from being with Richard. She wasn't about to let a bout of the flu keep her away from something she'd been anticipating for days. "I guess I did oversleep."

"Aren't you feeling well?"

Jenny sipped her orange juice as her grandmother's eagle eyes studied her. "It's summer. Can't I be lazy if I want?"

"You've never been lazy before. I've practically had to tie you down to keep you in the house during the summer."

"Maybe I'm changing. Maybe I like the idea of lying in bed until noon."

Marian smiled wryly. "And maybe cows will sprout wings and fly to the moon."

"Oh, Grandmother, stop worrying about me." Jenny spread honey on a piece of dry toast and hoped that she could force it down. She didn't want any more health questions from her grandmother. In truth, she was concerned about the way she'd been feeling lately. More unexplained bruises had popped out. One on her hip looked especially gruesome, yet she honestly couldn't remember banging into anything that might have caused it.

Her grandmother poured herself a cup of tea. "You know we'll be dining at the Club tonight."

"I haven't forgotten."

"It's the twenty-eighth wedding anniversary of the Holloways, and since Richard Senior has been my right hand in business all these years, this dinner is the least I can do to help them celebrate."

Jenny knew little of her grandmother's business affairs. She knew that her grandfather had died before she'd even been born, leaving control of his Boston bank to his wife. She knew that her father, Warren, their only child, whom she barely remembered, was supposed to have been their sole heir. But something had gone wrong between Warren and his mother, and he'd moved to London and married Jenny's mother, a British girl; together, they'd joined the Peace Corps. Jenny had been born in Uganda.

When she was seven, both her parents had died in a freak train wreck, and she'd come to the United States from Africa to live with her grandmother.

"I understand Richard's son will also be joining us," Jenny heard her grandmother say. "I trust you won't be too bored."

"No. He and I've been friends forever. I don't mind spending an evening with him."

"He's so much older than you."

"Four years isn't 'so much older,' " Jenny insisted. She felt her cheeks color when her grandmother gave her a penetrating stare.

"Is that all you're eating?" Grandmother changed the subject.

Jenny had placed the uneaten piece of toast onto her plate. "I don't want to spoil my appetite for dinner tonight."

"But that's hours from now."

"And I don't want to get fat."

"Hardly a problem," her grandmother said, eyeing Jenny carefully. "If anything, you've lost weight. Now, tell me you aren't going to turn into one of those self-centered girls who are always counting every calorie, are you?"

"You're not exactly a typical portly granny, you know," Jenny teased. Her grandmother was tall and slim and regal in her bearing. *True Bostonian nobility*, Richard had often remarked.

"Don't be impudent," Marian scolded, her blue eyes twinkling. " 'Portly'—the very idea! I'll have you know that none of my friends fit that kind of granny stereotype."

Jenny rose and dropped her linen napkin on her untouched plate of scrambled eggs. "And none of mine pig out when they know they're about to face a seven-course dinner. I've got some things to do today, and I need to get moving."

"But your breakfast—"

"See you later." Jenny dashed out of the room and into the hall. She made it to the staircase before a wave of nausea overtook her. She swayed, steadied herself, and groaned inwardly. She didn't want to be sick. She wanted to feel good and look good for Richard. She gripped the banister and slowly walked up the stairs. Maybe a little nap would help.

She went to her room and slid beneath the sheets of her canopy bed; in minutes, she fell into a fatigued and dreamless sleep.

Jenny felt no better by dinnertime. *But no worse either*, she insisted to herself as she dressed in a yellow sundress that dipped off her shoulders. She hoped that Richard would think her pretty and sophisticated, not simply the "kid next door." All through dinner, she struggled to keep her mind on the conversation, but found it difficult to concentrate.

"Why don't the two of you dance," Mrs. Holloway suggested, snapping Jenny out of her stupor. "No use being trapped at the table with us."

Jenny wished that Richard had asked her of his own accord, but decided not to quibble over the fine points. What did it matter how she ended up in Richard's arms, just so long as she did?

"Come on, Jenny." Richard stood and held out his hand.

Jenny felt her grandmother's gaze follow them to the dance floor, where she glided smoothly into Richard's arms. She thought she fit there perfectly.

"I don't think Dame Marian approves," Richard said.

"Of our dancing? Why shouldn't she?"

"I don't think she approves of *me*."

"Don't be silly. She likes you and always has."

"We're too old to be playmates," Richard cautioned.

Jenny didn't understand what he was trying to tell her. Perhaps he was feeling coerced into spending the evening with her, instead of out with a girl he really liked. "How's it going between you and your father?"

"Don't ask."

Richard seemed in a bad mood, which made her feel all the more like a nuisance. "Could we go out on the patio?" she asked. "It's stuffy in here."

He pulled back and studied her. "You look a little pale. Maybe we should sit down."

"Some fresh air should do it."

He led her outside onto a flagstone patio lined with stone benches and strings of colored lights. A faint breeze carried the scent of the sea. He took her to a bench near a low stone wall and settled her down.

She breathed in deeply, hoping the evening air would clear her head. Just her luck. A romantic corner in the moonlight with Richard, and she didn't feel well.

"Better?" he asked, sitting beside her and taking her hand.

Her pulse reacted to his touch. "Better," she said.

He loosened his tie and opened the collar of his shirt. "I'd rather be out sailing."

"Me too." She didn't add that sailing over a gentle sea under a star-studded sky alone with him would be her idea of heaven. "Maybe we could go out some morning next week."

"I don't think I can make it."

She bit back her disappointment. Why was he

avoiding her? She thought of other summers when they'd been inseparable. He was the one who'd taught her to sail. "You promised we would. Are you angry with me? Did I do something to offend you?"

"Of course not." He stood and paced to the wall and peered out into the darkness. "Dad wants me to be a runner in his firm this summer. He says it's time I learned to appreciate hard work."

Jenny knew that a runner was a lowly job that called on the employee to do detail work and odd jobs for attorneys in a law practice. "But you said you weren't interested in becoming a lawyer."

"I'm not, but it doesn't seem to matter to my father what I want to do. He won't listen to me. He's determined that I attend law school once I finish my undergraduate work."

"So that means you'll be working all summer?"

"Right up until the fall term starts. It also means he and I will be commuting to Boston for the summer."

Commuting meant that Richard would be living in the city during the week and only coming out to the island for weekends. Suddenly, her idyllic summer stretched in front of her like a long, lonely road. "Isn't there any way you can get out of it?"

"Only if I want to be cut loose from the family." Jenny stood, wanting to be closer to him, wanting to hold on to this slice of time in the moonlight. The movement was too quick, and she swayed. Richard caught her. "Hey, what's wrong? Are you ill?"

She felt lightheaded and clutched his arms for support. "I—I don't know ..."

The world around her tipped and swayed, and she felt as if she were tumbling into a deep well. Richard's arms lifted her as darkness engulfed her.

Three

❦

"How long have you been experiencing these symptoms, Miss Crawford?"

"I've been feeling sick for a few days," Jenny answered. She lay in the local emergency room while a doctor poked, prodded, and asked questions. She felt acutely embarrassed. It was bad enough to have fainted in Richard's arms, but it had caused a scene at the country club when the ambulance had come and picked her up. She knew her grandmother was beside herself out in the waiting room. At least the Holloways were with her. She grimaced, knowing that she'd spoiled their anniversary party.

"Did I hurt you?" the doctor asked as he rotated joints in her arms and legs.

"I'm a little sore," she confessed.

"And these bruises—how long have you had them?"

"I'm not sure. A couple of weeks. They just keep showing up. I guess I'm clumsier than I thought."

"I don't think you're clumsy," the doctor said.

"What do you think is wrong? Is it the flu?"

"Your lymph nodes are swollen, which indicates an infection of some kind." He patted her arm and smiled noncommittally. "We need to do some lab work."

"You mean stick needles in me?"

"We have to draw some blood, yes."

Jenny gritted her teeth. If there was one thing she hated, it was shots. She'd sobbed through every immunization as a child. "Then can I go home?"

"Actually, I think it wisest to check you in for observation."

"But I don't want to stay here!"

"It'll only be a for a few days—until we figure out what's going on with you."

Jenny saw her summer fun evaporating. First, Richard wouldn't be around, and now this. Why was this happening to her?

A nurse stepped around the curtain that shut Jenny off from others in the emergency care area and prepared her arm to take blood. "Relax," the nurse said.

Jenny shut her eyes and promised herself she'd be brave, but the sharp sting of the needle into her vein made tears well up. She hated to act like a baby over a needle and hoped the nurse didn't see them. "All done," the nurse said, taping a cotton ball to the inside of Jenny's arm. "Hold it tight, or you'll get a bad bruise."

"What's one more going to matter?" Jenny muttered.

The doctor reappeared with her grandmother in tow. "I'm making arrangements for you to go upstairs," he told Jenny. "As I've told your grandmother, ours is a small hospital with minimal equipment."

"How much equipment will I need?"

He smiled and made notations on a clipboard. "Nothing for the night. Don't worry. We'll take good care of you."

"I want Jenny to be comfortable," Grandmother said. "I want her in your best room."

"Grandmother, please, it's not necessary."

"I'll be contacting my personal physician in Boston first thing in the morning." Marian cast a challenging eye toward the ER doctor. "I want to be certain that Jenny gets special attention. I don't want anything to be missed or overlooked."

"If it's necessary for her to return to Boston, we will recommend it," the doctor replied.

Return to Boston! Jenny reacted instantly. "But it's summer. I always spend summers here. I don't want to go back to the city." Then she remembered that Richard also would be in Boston, and her plight didn't seem so terrible.

"I must do what's best for you," her grandmother said. "If you must return, I shall too. I'll have the staff reopen the house and close up the one here."

"But it's your summer too."

"Why, I wouldn't dream of sending you back to the city while I remained behind. It's out of the question."

Deep down, Jenny was relieved. She wanted her grandmother with her. Marian had been a substitute mother to Jenny for nine years, and Jenny didn't want to face hospitalization all alone.

"Your room's ready," the doctor told her, when a nurse handed him a piece of paper. "You've got a

private room on the third floor, one of our largest."
Jenny wondered if he expected her to feel grateful.

"Perhaps I should stay also," Grandmother offered.

"There aren't any facilities for guests," the doctor answered.

"Grandmother, don't," Jenny interrupted. "I'm not a baby." Although Marian was very fit for her age, she was sixty-six, and Jenny felt concerned about her. She would be more comfortable in her own home, in her own bed. "You can be here first thing in the morning."

"We've given your granddaughter a little something to help her sleep," the doctor added. "She'll sleep through the night, and we'll begin tests in the morning."

Grandmother looked skeptical, but agreed. Minutes later, an orderly helped Jenny into a wheelchair and pushed her toward the elevator. In the hallway, Jenny saw the Holloways and Richard. "Oh, you poor dear," Dorothy Holloway exclaimed.

Jenny hardly heard her, for it was the stricken, frightened expression on Richard's face that held her attention. "Are you all right?" He dropped to his knees in front of the wheelchair and took her hand.

"I don't know. They're running some tests tomorrow."

"They're insisting Jenny stay the night," Marian explained. "I hate for her to be alone."

"She won't be," Richard replied. "I'll stay with her."

Jenny felt embarrassed. Grandmother's hint was so broad that a three-year-old could have picked up on it. Of course, Richard had no choice but to offer to spend the night. She sighed, too tired and achy to argue that it wasn't necessary.

The group of them entered the elevator, then the quiet hall of the third floor. A nurse led the way to the room, where she helped Jenny change into a hospital gown and get into bed. The sheets felt cool, and Jenny pulled up the covers gratefully. Once she was settled, the others came in to say good-night.

"I've made arrangements for a phone to be placed in your room," Grandmother told Jenny. "If you want anything, call me."

"I'll be fine." Jenny had never been inside a hospital before, and even though this one was small and homey, she didn't like it. The smells of disinfectants and antiseptics repelled her.

"I'll keep checking on her," Richard insisted. "There's a visitors' lounge just down the hall where I can spend the night."

Grandmother kissed her, and Jenny said good-bye to Richard's parents, then breathed a sigh of relief when she was finally alone with Richard. "They were making me nervous," she said.

"They're just worried."

She realized that the hospital gown was not very attractive, and suddenly, in spite of how bad she was feeling, she cared about how Richard saw her. "Thanks for catching me out on the patio. I owe you one."

"You looked very pretty tonight," he said, touching her cheek.

She caught his hand and pressed it against her skin. "I'm scared, Richard. I don't like being sick."

"Maybe it's just the flu."

"If it were, they'd have sent me home."

"You're Jenny Crawford—they wouldn't take any chances."

His explanation didn't wash, but she was starting to feel numb from the pill they'd given her in ER. "Will you stay with me until I fall asleep?"

"I'm not going anywhere."

Richard watched her eyelids flutter closed and her breathing grow deep and regular, yet he held tightly to her hand even after her grip on his relaxed. She'd scared him when she'd passed out. He was still shaking from the ordeal. Something was wrong with her. Something serious. He felt it in his gut. Perfectly healthy sixteen-year-old girls didn't sprout bruises on their bodies and keel over for no reason.

Cool it, he told himself. She didn't need him going crazy on her. There had to be a reasonable medical explanation. He brushed the backs of his fingers down her cheek. "Jenny . . ." he whispered. "Be okay."

He bent forward, smoothed her hair off her forehead, and kissed her tenderly. He stepped backward, his gaze never leaving her sleeping face. He sighed, recalled seeing a coffee machine in the lounge, and headed toward it. It was going to be a long night.

Four

JENNY WAS AWAKENED before dawn by the rattle of glass tubes and syringes carried into her room by a technician. "We need a little blood," the tech said.

Still groggy, Jenny struggled to remember where she was and why. The memory of the night before returned like a bad dream. "Richard?" She looked around the room, feeling panicked.

He was coming through the door with a cup of coffee. "What's going on?" he asked the tech sharply.

"The lab needs a blood sample."

Jenny reached out her hand, and Richard took it. He stepped between Jenny and the tech. "Can you give her a minute? You woke her from a sound sleep."

"I've got to keep on schedule. She's not the only one I've got to see this morning. It's part of the routine."

Jenny didn't like the tone of reprimand she heard

in the older woman's voice. It may be routine for the tech, but it was far from routine for her. "It's all right," she assured Richard, feeling him tense. "Just hold my hand while she sticks me."

"That's not customary," the tech started.

"Today, make it customary," Richard replied.

The tech sized them both up, pressed her lips together, and shrugged. She sorted through her tubes and prepared Jenny's arm for the syringe. Jenny stared into the depths of Richard's green eyes while the needle stuck and stung her arm.

Once the tech had gone, Richard leaned over her bed. "You doing all right?"

"Maybe it'll get easier over time."

"Maybe this will be the last time."

She hoped so. "Thank you for staying the night. Sorry I wasn't much company."

"This wasn't supposed to be a house party." He smiled. "The last time I saw the sun come up, I was in the Bahamas on a sailboat."

"I wish that's where we were right now. Was it beautiful?"

"I can't even describe it."

His hair was falling over his forehead, and a stubble of beard outlined his chin and jaw. Although he looked rumpled and tired, Jenny thought he looked very sexy. "We never did get to go sailing."

"When they let you out of here, it's the first thing we'll do," Richard promised.

"How was your night in the lounge?" she asked.

"Green vinyl chairs with metal arms will never replace featherbeds as bedroom furniture."

She giggled. "That bad, huh?"

He rubbed the small of his back. "I didn't even

know I had muscles to cramp where that chair found them."

"It's all right with me if you go on home now. I'll be perfectly fine until Grandmother arrives."

"No way." He swallowed a last gulp of coffee from a Styrofoam cup. "I told your grandmother I'd stay with you, and I will."

He stayed because he promised Grandmother, Jenny told herself. *Not because of me.* "Is there a place for you to eat breakfast?"

"There's a coffee shop downstairs, a newspaper box, and a hole in the wall that passes for a gift shop."

"It sounds as if you've explored the whole building."

"There's not much to explore. The place is small." He fiddled with the Styrofoam cup, chipping out little pieces and piling them up on her bedside table. "How are you feeling this morning?"

"Better now that the blood work's over. Thanks for holding my hand. I really hate shots."

"Me too," he confessed. "What about your other symptoms? How are you feeling from them?"

She took a quick inventory, rotating her ankles and wrists slowly. "I still ache all over, and I've got a slight headache, but that might be left over from the sleeping pill. I feel pretty groggy."

"I think I hear someone bringing breakfast trays," Richard said, crossing to the door. He looked down the hall and announced, "Here they come."

Jenny's stomach revolted as the smell of greasy bacon and eggs drifted into her room. A minute later, an orderly plopped a tray on a table that straddled her bed. She edged up the lid, peeked at the contents, and heard Richard chuckle. "Are you afraid there's a live snake under there?"

"I'd rather face one than this stuff."

He removed the lid, and together they stared at the unappetizing offering. "It looks grim all right. How about some Frosted Flakes?" He indicated a small box of cereal and a carton of milk. "They look sealed. How can you go wrong with cereal?"

"I could try them." Richard prepared the bowl for her. She took several bites, but shoved it aside before finishing. "That's all I can eat," she said. "Do you think Tony the Tiger will forgive me?"

"I'll speak to him personally." Richard recovered the tray and took it into the hall. "I've got to speak to someone about the room service in this place."

"Silly." She offered him a smile. It was good having him with her, even if he was only doing it for her grandmother's sake. "I wonder when they're going to start on the tests the doctor mentioned in ER last night."

"Do you want me to go find out?"

"If you don't mind."

He gave a brisk salute. "Private Holloway at your service." The sound of her laugh followed him down the hall to the nurses' station, where he asked the nurse behind the desk what was happening with Jenny's tests.

The nurse rifled through some papers. "There's a hold order on her case."

"Meaning?"

"Meaning that her family has requested that nothing be done until another doctor's been called in for a consultation."

Richard pondered the news. Marian Crawford

must be seeking a specialist for Jenny. He thought it was a good idea, but it also made him feel uneasy. What kind of specialist, he wondered. His watch indicated that it was eight A.M. He'd half expected Marian to have arrived by now. Something was going on; he wished he knew what.

He had checked on Jenny throughout the long night, sleeping in spurts, and although she had slept soundly, he could tell by looking at her that she wasn't any better. He was positive that she'd valiantly attempted breakfast only because he'd forced the issue.

When he returned to Jenny's room, he found that she'd fallen back to sleep. He was relieved, because he didn't have anything to tell her and he didn't want her to worry about torturous tests that probably involved needles and unsympathetic lab technicians.

An hour later, she was still asleep and he was reading the morning paper in the lounge when the elevator opened and Marian Crawford stepped out.

"How's Jenny?" she asked anxiously. Concern lined her face, and in spite of her fresh appearance, Richard guessed that she'd not slept much either the night before.

"Jenny had a good night. She's sleeping now."

"Thank you for staying with her."

"I stayed because I wanted to."

She lifted an eyebrow, but he didn't flinch. "I've been on the phone half the night with my personal physician in Boston and several specialists he recommended."

Richard pictured doctors all over Boston being

routed out of bed in the middle of the night to take Dame Marian's calls. "What's going on?"

"We're flying back to Boston this afternoon."

His stomach tightened. "Where will you put her?"

"In Boston Children's Hospital. It's the best facility in the region for her perceived medical problem."

An alarm went off in Richard's head. "They know what's wrong with her?"

"I insisted that the results of last night's lab work be sent directly to my doctor. He called me at midnight, and we made the decision to move her."

Richard felt suddenly alert as adrenaline pumped through him. All his life, he'd thought Marian very intimidating, knowing her to be a tough businesswoman, but also soft as a marshmallow when it came to Jenny. He'd always shown her deference, yet now he refused to be cowed by her. "Mrs. Crawford, please tell me what's going on. Tell me what's wrong with Jenny."

She didn't speak immediately, as if she was weighing her options. Finally, she said, "Last night, Jenny's white blood count was over two hundred thousand."

He wished he'd paid more attention during biology class. "I'm sorry, I don't know what that means."

"I didn't either. I asked and was told that normal is about ten thousand."

He gave a low whistle. "She's twenty times normal."

"I had my physician call the ER doctor, and afterward, when we discussed their conversation, he suggested that I get her to a specialist as quickly as possible."

"A specialist at Boston Children's," Richard said with a nod. "What kind of specialist?"

"A pediatric oncologist."

Before Richard could ask, Jenny's grandmother told him, "A cancer specialist," Marian's voice caught. "They believe Jenny has leukemia."

Five

~~

"LEUKEMIA?" THE WORD tasted foreign on his tongue, and he didn't like it.

"It's a type of cancer of the blood." Richard knew what leukemia was. Marian continued, her voice trembling and her face lined with worry. "They've told me there are several kinds, so her specific variety must be determined by specific testing. Children's Hospital is the foremost facility in the Northeast for treating cancer in the young."

"Cancer? Jenny has cancer?" Richard felt as if he'd been hurled against a stone wall.

"Very probably."

"But . . . but that's impossible." He couldn't absorb it, couldn't accept it.

"I've spent the longest night of my life over this," Marian said. "I'm prepared for the worst, but I'm holding out hope that her problem can be explained in some other way."

He shook his head. "I don't know what to say . . ."

"Don't say anything," Marian directed in her best no-nonsense tone. "Especially to Jenny. She must not know what she's being tested for."

Richard jerked up his head and leveled a long look at Marian. "You can't hide the truth from her."

"I can, and I will. And so will you." Her shoulders slumped slightly, and she continued in a kinder voice. "There's no need to alarm her at this point. After all the test results are in at Children's, then I will do whatever her oncologist recommends."

Richard agreed with her logic. Of course, there was no need to say anything to Jenny at this stage. If it was a mistake, then no harm would have to be undone. Why, they might actually laugh about it. He'd take her sailing and tease her with, "Remember the time they thought you had cancer?"

She would laugh and say, "How could they have been so dumb? Imagine, a few bruises and a high white blood count, and they misdiagnose leukemia."

If it was true—Richard halted his train of thought. It couldn't be true. "What do you want me to do, Mrs. Crawford?"

"I want you to act as if you know nothing."

"Won't she wonder what's going on when you head back to Boston?"

"Probably. But I intend to continue playing the eccentric old grandmother who won't allow local medical personnel to handle my beloved grand-daughter's case. She'll accept that. She's seen me in action before."

Richard felt a grudging respect for the woman. She was sharp and clever, and most of all, she loved Jenny with a vengeance. Nothing would get past her when it came to any treatment that Jenny might need. "I'll help however I can. In fact, I'll fly over with you."

"That's one sure way to tip her off," Marian replied. "She will expect you to stay put if there's nothing seriously wrong with her."

"Jenny knows I'm due at my father's law offices at nine o'clock Monday morning to start work. I wasn't planning to show up."

"You were going to defy your father?" Marian looked aghast.

"I wasn't going to let him force me into doing something I didn't want to do."

She gave a short, cryptic laugh. "Yes, I heard the same words from my own son, Jenny's father, some eighteen years ago."

Warren Crawford had defied his mother? Richard thought the information amazing. He returned to his original train of thought by saying, "My decision not to show up has changed now. So long as Jenny's in the hospital in Boston, I'll stay in the city and work for my father. I'm pretty sure he'll give me time off to visit her whenever I want."

Marian looked as if she might say something about his plans, but for some reason, she changed her mind. She straightened and turned to leave the visitors' lounge. "I'm going to check on Jenny now. I've already informed the administration that I'll be moving her to Children's. Our flight leaves at four this afternoon. I only hope I can convince her that this move is purely routine."

Routine. It was the second time that morning he'd heard the word. A sixteen-year-old girl with her whole life ahead of her may be about to learn she has cancer—what could possibly be routine about that? Richard clenched his fists. "I'll call home and let mother know my plans. She can pack my things and probably get me on the same flight."

"Very well," Marian said. Richard couldn't help noticing that her inflection sounded more like permission than acceptance.

Jenny felt as if a curtain of secrecy had descended around her while her grandmother busied herself with plans for returning to Boston. Even Richard seemed to be a part of the conspiracy of silence. While she was thrilled to know he'd be coming to Boston with them that afternoon, he was acting far too casual about returning in order to work for his father's law firm. She remembered how angry he'd been about it at the country club. Was there more going on than he and Grandmother were telling her?

They left the hospital and rode in Grandmother's Lincoln to the airport, where the chauffeur unloaded their bags and they boarded a plane for the bumpy flight over the water to the metropolitan Boston area. Another chauffeured car met them and took them directly to Children's Hospital.

Jenny felt overwhelmed by the enormous facility, so totally different from the tiny community hospital on Martha's Vineyard. The new hospital soared ten stories and sprawled over two city blocks. Once inside, she was whisked up to a top floor and ushered into a private room with windows overlooking downtown Boston. The room held not only a bed, but a sofa, TV, and stocked refrigerator.

"Grandmother!" Jenny exclaimed. "This place looks like a hotel suite."

"Money can buy some amenities, dear. I want you to be comfortable."

Richard caught Jenny's eye and flashed her a look that said, *Don't fight it.*

"I really don't need all this."

"Nonsense. This ordeal is stressful enough."

"I didn't know hospitals had rooms like this," Richard commented. "Especially a kids' hospital."

"Children of celebrities become ill too," Marian replied, opening dresser drawers. "Did you think they weren't given preferential treatment?"

"I'm not the queen of England."

Marian brushed off Jenny's remark. "Your doctor will be in later this evening to meet you. His name is Jason Gallagher, and I'm assured he's one of the best."

"The best for what?"

Marian barely missed a beat before answering, "The best diagnostician in the area. He'll get to the bottom of what's ailing you."

"So I will have to go through a bunch of awful tests after all."

"I'm afraid so." Marian took Jenny's hand and squeezed it. "Don't worry. I'll be with you through each one of them. And so will Mrs. Kelly."

"Who's that?"

"The private-duty nurse I've hired to stay with you."

Jenny glanced furtively toward Richard. Of course, it would be impossible for him to remain with her. He looked dead on his feet anyway.

"I'll be over to see you as soon as I get off work tomorrow," he told her.

"Why don't you get into bed, my dear," Grandmother said. "You must be exhausted."

She *was* tired. She felt sick again too. The doctor at the other hospital had given her plenty of medication, but the effects had worn off. Richard stepped out of the room, and she changed into a white lacy cotton nightgown her grandmother had purchased for her. "Nothing like something new to make a girl feel good," Grandmother remarked cheerfully. "You look very pretty, Jenny."

"I look awful," Jenny said. "The gown looks very pretty." She snuggled beneath the crisp, clean sheets. "I wish I were home."

"Me too." Grandmother kissed her cheek. "You get some rest, and I'll see to it that Richard gets to his place. He's had a long couple of days."

Suddenly, Jenny didn't want to be left alone. "You'll be back?"

"Absolutely. I want to meet this highly touted young doctor who's supposed to take care of you."

"Be nice to him, Grandmother."

"Don't lecture me, dear. I expect top performances from the people I hire."

Jenny sighed in exasperation. "Sometimes you have to play by other people's rules."

Grandmother scoffed and unpacked Jenny's things.

When Jenny was finally alone, she hated it. The room was too big, too quiet. As if in response to her yearning for company, the door swung open and a woman dressed in a white uniform entered. "Hi, I'm Alice," she said. "I've come to draw a little blood for the lab boys." Jenny swallowed hard. For a moment, she'd forgotten where she was. "Are you Jenny?"

"Yes." Her eyes grew wide at the sight of the needle.

"I'm really pretty good," Alice said sympathetically. "Some people tell me they don't feel a thing."

Jenny wanted Richard with her, then realized that even if he were, she'd still have to give *her* blood. She bravely held out her arm. *Lesson number one,* she told herself. *Some things you have to do on your own.*

Six

LATER THAT NIGHT, Jenny met Dr. Gallagher. He was a large man with flyaway copper-red hair, freckles, and a big, booming voice filled with enthusiasm. Jenny liked him instantly. "I want you to know, Jenny, that I'm absolutely honest with my patients. I won't lie to you, and I won't hide information. But I also expect my patients to level with me and do what I tell them."

Taken aback, Jenny nodded. Why would she have a reason to lie to him? And why would a doctor conceal information? "I'll try," she said.

"I'm sending you down for a battery of tests starting first thing in the morning. Some won't be too pleasant, others will be a snap. Once the results are analyzed, I'll give you a full report and map out a medical protocol for you. Fair enough?"

Bewildered, she nodded. She didn't even know what they were testing her for. She started to ask, but her grandmother entered the room with an older woman, the private-duty nurse, Mrs. Kelly, and Dr. Gallagher hurried off to see other patients. "I wanted to talk to him," Jenny told her grandmother.

"He'll have a long consultation with you when the test results are in," Grandmother assured her with a smile that never made it to her saddened eyes.

The next morning, after her blood work, Jenny was taken down to radiology for a round of X rays and then to a room with a lab table. Dr. Gallagher greeted her as he pulled on latex gloves. "Hop up," a young intern assisting him said.

"Why?"

"We're going to do a bone marrow aspiration."

"What's that?"

Dr. Gallagher explained, "I told you last night I would be open with you, and I will. We're going to put you on your stomach with a pillow under your hips. I'll paint some Betadine—that's an iodine-based antiseptic solution—on the skin to kill bacteria, then I'll give you a little shot to numb the area. Next, I'll insert a special syringe through the skin, into the pelvic bone, and draw out some bone marrow."

Jenny gasped. If she could have jumped off the table and fled the room, she would have. "Will it hurt?"

"You'll feel a sensation of pressure, maybe some pain. It's different for every patient. But I won't take long, so it will be over quickly. Maybe five minutes."

The five minutes seemed like an eternity to Jenny. She tried to ignore the smells and sounds, refusing to watch the procedure by keeping her gaze focused on a small dark stain on the wall in front of her. She attempted to keep track of Dr. Gallagher's rambling, constant conversation, but when she felt the pressure deep inside her hip, the pulling sensation as the spongy marrow of her bones was sucked into a needle, she felt nauseated and lightheaded. For a second, she thought she might pass out.

"All done," Dr. Gallagher announced. "You did well, Jenny." He patted her arm, and she let out her breath and blinked back tears. "You'll probably be sore there for a few days, so take it easy."

"Now what?" she asked.

"Now I send everything to the lab. We'll have some definite answers by tomorrow."

At the end of a grueling day, Jenny was glad to be back in her room, even though she was lonely. Mrs. Kelly was nice enough, but Jenny didn't have much in common with her. When Richard showed up right after supper, Jenny threw her arms around him.

"Nice greeting," he said, hugging her in return.

Self-conscious about her childlike display of affection, Jenny pulled away. "They stuck needles into my bones, Richard."

He blanched. "I'm sorry."

"I hate it here, and no one's telling me anything."

He glanced about evasively. "I'm sure they'll tell you everything once the results are in."

"It's my body. It's *me* this is happening to. Why won't they tell me anything?" Richard paced to the window and stared gloomily out onto the city below. Jenny caught herself and said, "I don't mean to take it out on you. It's just been a long day."

"You can take it out on me all you want," he said moodily.

She sighed. "Let's start over. Come here and tell me about your first day on the job."

He came back to her bedside, but she could tell he was tense and uneasy. "It went all right. My father was in court most of the day, so one of the junior partners took me under his wing. I've got a lot of research to do in the law library for a case he's prosecuting."

"Looks like neither one of us is doing what we wanted to do this summer."

He reached out and brushed her cheek. "So it seems."

Just his touch set butterflies into motion in her stomach. "When they figure out what's wrong and I get out of this place, we'll go spend an afternoon in our cave, all right?"

"All right." Their gazes held. Richard hated himself for keeping the truth from her. Why had he made such a promise to her grandmother? Why didn't Marian realize that sooner or later, Jenny would discover the truth and maybe hate them both for keeping it from her? He cleared his throat. "I should be going."

"You just got here." She looked hurt. Richard was afraid to stay much longer. He was afraid he'd blurt out something he shouldn't.

"I'll be back tomorrow when I can stay longer." *Besides,* he told himself, *by tomorrow, she might know the truth.*

Marian came by right after Richard left. "What's the problem?"

"I'm not having much fun."

Grandmother smiled wistfully. "When you were a child, you used to tell me that on days it would rain and you couldn't go the beach."

Jenny felt as if her whole life was being rained on

at the moment. "Do you know what's going on with all these tests yet?" she asked.

"Not yet." Grandmother's mouth said one thing, but her eyes said another.

"You do know, but you won't tell me," Jenny accused. When Jenny had first come to live with her grandmother, she had been in awe of Marian, who seemed very stern and businesslike—not at all like the affectionate mother who had kissed her, climbed on a train, and never come home.

Jenny hadn't been living with her grandmother long when Marian came in her bedroom and discovered her sobbing beneath her covers. Right then, Marian had taken her into her arms and held her. "I do love you, Jenny," she confessed. "I'm sorry I've not made you feel more welcome, less lonely. Please forgive me."

It wasn't until Jenny was quite a bit older that she'd begun to appreciate what an upheaval her unexpected entrance had caused in her grandmother's life. In a week's time, Marian had learned that her son was dead and that she was going to have to raise his daughter because there were no other relatives to take the child.

Jenny had grown up with life's fine things—two houses, beautiful clothes, the best prep schools, but those things mattered little to her. Perhaps because she'd lost her parents when she'd been so young, what mattered most to her were the people in her life. Her grandmother, her few friends, Richard. More and more, Richard.

"Jenny," Grandmother said, lifting her hand from the white sheet of the hospital bed. "When there is something to tell you, we will tell you. Until then, rest and keep your strength."

Jenny nodded her acceptance, but like a condemned prisoner, she wasn't sure where she'd find the courage to face the dawn and whatever it held about her future.

She was toying with the food on her breakfast tray and feeling awful when Dr. Gallagher arrived at seven the next morning. Surprised to see him so early, Jenny pushed the tray aside. Even more surprising was seeing her grandmother right beside him. The expressions on their faces told her that the two of them had been discussing her.

"It's bad, isn't it?" Jenny's gaze darted from face to face.

"I told you I'd always level with you," Dr. Gallagher said kindly.

"Yes, you did." Jenny took hold of her grandmother's offered hand. "What's wrong with me?"

"The tests confirm that you have leukemia, Jenny. A particularly vicious and complicated form of leukemia."

Seven

AT FIRST, THE words didn't sink in. *Leukemia.* "That's a kind of cancer, isn't it?" She felt her grandmother's hand tighten on hers.

"Yes," Dr. Gallagher said. "What happens is that for reasons no one can explain, a single white blood cell in your bone marrow goes crazy. This mutant cell begins to multiply like wildfire and crowds out normal red blood cells. You become anemic—that's why you've felt tired and listless. Your lymph glands and spleen swell. Yet, your white blood cells are immature, and as they begin to infiltrate your bloodstream and organs, you develop bruises and unexplained fevers."

Jenny felt detached and numb, as if they weren't discussing her at all. "Don't people die from leukemia?" she asked.

"Not if I can help it," Dr. Gallagher replied. "This is 1978, Jenny. In the fifties and sixties, this disease couldn't be checked, but we know more about it today. We have some very potent chemotherapy—drugs to kill off the mutant cells. We use radiation treatments, cortisones, an arsenal of medications."

Jenny felt icy cold with fear. Tears began to slide down her cheeks.

"We're going to fight this thing," her grandmother said, taking hold of her shoulders. "If it takes every penny in my bank account, every cent set aside in your trust fund, we'll spend it. Nothing's more important than your getting well, my dear Jenny. Nothing."

Jenny longed to feel positive about her prospects, but she was so weak, so ill that she couldn't sort it all out. How could she have possibly gotten leukemia? Why had her body turned on her this way?

"The first thing we'll do," Dr. Gallagher explained, "is give you a blood transfusion, which will make you feel better immediately. Next, I'll start you on a chemo protocol and try and get this disease into remission."

"Remission?"

"That's a halt to the progression of the disease. Once it's achieved, you can go home, and you'll only have to come in for periodic blood work and chemo sessions."

Home! Had a word ever sounded more beautiful to her? Jenny reached for a tissue. "All right. I'll do whatever you want me to do."

"That's a girl," the doctor said.

He left to write up the order for her transfusion, promising to check in on her later. "I'm scared, Grandmother. I don't want to go through this."

"I'm scared too," the older woman confessed. "But you just remember, you're from good Yankee stock." Marian offered a slight smile. "I was a

Winston-Cabot, and your grandfather a Crawford. Our ancestors came over on the Mayflower and carved a living out of the solid granite of Massachusetts—no easy task. You can lick this thing."

"How long have you known?" Jenny asked. "You didn't want me to know, did you?"

"Not until they were positive. There seemed no sense in worrying you."

"Please don't ever do that to me again."

Marian gave Jenny a startled look. "Whatever do you mean?"

"You should have told me what they suspected. You had no right to hold back the truth."

"There was no truth until today. It seemed pointless to let you worry over what could have been a false alarm."

"But I had a right to know. Richard knows, doesn't he?"

Grandmother's cheeks flushed. "He knows what was suspected, but he doesn't know about the positive lab results."

"I want to tell him," Jenny said.

Grandmother started to protest, but decided against it, telling Jenny, "Very well. But please don't be angry with me. I was only trying to protect you."

Seeing the pain on her grandmother's face, Jenny felt a wave of forgiveness sweep through her. "How old was my father when he moved to London?"

"Warren was nineteen when he left home."

"That's only three years older than me."

"Why is that important to you?"

Jenny wasn't sure. She only knew that somehow, in the last half hour she'd passed from the world of childhood into the realm of adult. The passage had been quick and stunning and harsh, without time for even a backward glance. "Maybe because I always thought when I was grown, I would understand why he and Mother died. It must be in the same category as why people get cancer."

Grandmother opened her arms and pulled Jenny into them. "I have no answers for you, my dear. Except to say that if I could have died in my son's place, I would have. And if I could have this disease in your place, I would get it."

Together, the two of them wept until a nurse entered, bringing an IV stand and two plastic bags of rich, red, healthy blood for Jenny.

The transfusion took several hours, but Dr. Gallagher had been correct in predicting that she would feel better. By that evening, Jenny felt revitalized. "Now I know how vampires feel after they've sunk their fangs into a victim's neck," Jenny told the nurse who came to check and regulate the flow of the blood.

With the IV line taped to her arm, Jenny attempted to put on makeup before Richard arrived. She wanted him to see her looking pretty again instead of sickly. "You look great," he told her when he came into the room.

"The tests came back," Jenny informed him, without preamble. "I have leukemia."

His eyes closed, and he rocked back on his heels as if he'd been shoved by some invisible hand.

She didn't want him feeling pity, so she continued matter-of-factly, "I'll be starting chemotherapy tomorrow morning. I don't know much about it yet, except that it's unpleasant. I—I think it might be best if you don't come visit for a while."

"What? Why not?"

She was fibbing to him. She'd read about the side effects of chemo and talked to the nurses about it. She would get sick—deathly sick. At some point, she'd lose her hair, and she'd probably develop skin lesions and grow weak and disoriented as the poisons potent enough to kill the cancer cells killed healthy cells as well. The cortisone would make her face and limbs swell with retained water. The radiation would make her nauseated and ill. She didn't want him to see her that way. "It's what I want, Richard," Jenny said quietly.

"But I want to be with you."

"You can have a good time in Boston. You don't need to hang around this place. You can sail over to Martha's Vineyard on the weekends. Isn't that girl there? You know, the one from Vassar you told me about?"

He said nothing, giving her the courage to continue. "You shouldn't have to ruin your summer running back and forth to the hospital. It'll be all right if you call me. I still want to keep in touch. I want to hear about your job and things like that."

"How can you ask me to stay away? I don't want you going through this all by yourself."

"Grandmother will be with me. And Mrs. Kelly."

"But not me."

He made it sound like an accusation. She struggled against a flood of emotions. She wanted him with her more than anything, but she couldn't tell him. "When it's over," she said carefully, "when I go into remission and go home, then I'll make plans with you. Then you can take me sailing."

Richard's insides felt cold and hard. She was shutting him out! He kept seeing her as a little girl by the side of her parents' graves. He had been the one to persuade her to leave the cemetery and go with her grandmother in the black limousine. "*I don't want to leave them,*" she had cried when he'd knelt down beside her.

"*You can't stay,*" he'd told her. "*Come on with me. We'll be friends.*" Now, it was she who was telling him he couldn't stay. "Jenny, please don't do this. I want to see you through this thing."

"I'd rather you see me after it's over." She gave a small laugh. "I made a joke." The smile faded, and she stared at him. "Please, do what I ask."

"You're not being fair." He backed toward the door, angry, agitated. "This isn't over."

"Call me," she said as the door swung open. "Call me," she whispered as it shut behind him.

Alone in the huge private room, Jenny trembled. She'd sent Richard away. *It's for the best,* she insisted. Wasn't everyone doing what was "best"? Her grandmother thought it best to protect her by holding back the truth. The doctor's best was an attempt to heal her by pumping her full of chemicals and drugs. She was trying her best to handle what was happening to her without falling apart.

The aching emptiness inside her felt like a bottomless well. All her plans and dreams drifted away like smoke. And worst of all, she felt utterly and completely alone. Sure, Grandmother and the doctor would help her. But she was the one who had to endure the pain, the treatments, the loss of all her dreams. How could they truly understand what she was going through? How could anyone?

Jenny curled up on the bed and wept, not only for what she was losing, but for what she might never have.

Eight

NOTHING PREPARED JENNY for chemotherapy—not the reading material the nurses gave her, not descriptions of it from the nurses themselves. The chemo room was located several floors below Jenny's private room. It was painted a soft green color and contained several contour chairs, each with a metal IV stand beside it. There was a TV set in the room, racks of magazines on the walls, a toy chest, and a fully stocked pantry. She noticed that there were no windows, and wondered if windows had been eliminated for fear that someone might try to crash through one in an attempt to escape.

Jenny stretched out on the curved chair, and when a nurse offered her an assortment of magazines, she experienced a sense of melancholy. Some of the titles were for small children, and it struck her profoundly that little ones, kids much younger than she, had to face this same ordeal.

"Ready?" a nurse named Lois asked.

"I guess so," Jenny mumbled, although her brain screamed, *Never*! She was glad that when her grandmother had asked to come to the session with Jenny, Dr. Gallagher had said, "Jenny's an adult. This is her disease. You'll be needed later, after she returns to her room." Instinctively, Jenny knew this was something no one could help her do. She must go down this road alone.

Lois prepped Jenny's arm for the needle that would be inserted into her vein so that the powerful chemicals could drip slowly into her bloodstream. "The treatment takes about forty-five minutes," Lois said. "If you need anything, just holler. I'll be right over there at my desk."

Jenny nodded and swallowed a lump of fear. She felt the tip of the needle slide into her flesh, and Lois tape it down. Her heart hammered. *The worst is over*, she told herself, attempting to relax.

Lois adjusted valves on tubing leading from two plastic bags on the IV stand and patted Jenny's shoulder. "This will regulate the flow." The nurse stepped away.

Panic seized Jenny as the first dose of medicine hit her system, for it burned like liquid fire. The sensation was so intense that she stared at her arm, certain that it would burst into flames. Suddenly, extreme nausea gripped her. Her stomach heaved, and she choked back bile.

Instantly, Lois was at her side. "Feeling a little shaky?" Lois handed her a beige plastic basin. "Don't hold back. If you want to throw up, do it."

Horrified, Jenny grabbed the basin, struggled in vain against the relentless waves of nausea, and finally gave in to them. She vomited over and over. Each time, Lois emptied the basin, washed Jenny's face, and handed the basin back to her. Soon, Jenny was trembling and shaking from head to toe. Tears ran down her cheeks. How could she endure this torture?

"You will adjust," Lois said softly.

All Jenny could do was silently beg God to let it be over—even if it meant dying right that moment.

Jenny didn't die, but when the procedure was over, she was so weak that she had to be lifted onto a gurney for the return trip to her room. Once she was back in her bed, Mrs. Kelly and her grandmother fussed over her, and even though Jenny could see how pinched and white her grandmother's face appeared, she could offer no words to comfort her.

"Don't think about the bad parts," Mrs. Kelly counseled as she placed a cool compress on the back of Jenny's neck. "Think about how millions of cancer cells are dying inside your body because of the medicine. Think about how the chemo is hunting them down in your bloodstream and blasting them into oblivion."

Jenny tried to focus on the positive, but had trouble. Yes, the bad were being destroyed, but what of her good cells? Weren't they in danger too? How could she endure this kind of agony three times a week? She closed her eyes, certain that if the cancer didn't kill her, the treatments would.

"Why can't I see her? Why won't she let me be with her?" Richard paced on the fine Oriental carpet in front of the ornate Louis XIV desk in Marian Crawford's Boston mansion. Marian sat ramrod straight behind the desk, allowing him to vent his frustration. "I won't upset her, Mrs. Crawford. All I want to do is see her. It's been over three weeks."

"Richard, please try and understand how physically and emotionally demanding her chemotherapy regime is. She's really not up to having any visitors."

"Visitors?" Richard fairly spat the word. "I'm not a visitor, Mrs. Crawford. I'm her friend. We've practically grown up together."

"Then all the more reason for you to accept her wishes."

"What about my wishes? Don't you know how crazy it's making me not to be able to even *see* her?"

Marian stood abruptly, pressed her palms against the top of the desk, and leaned toward him. "This isn't about *you*, Richard. For the time being, you will not be allowed to see her."

Taken aback by her angry tone, Richard stopped pacing and turned to face Jenny's grandmother. "You can't stop me," he said carefully.

"I can, and I will. I will post a security guard beside her door, and no one will be allowed entrance except medical personnel."

"You'd go that far to keep me away from her?" He'd heard his father say that no one ever opposed Marian's will and lived to tell about it. Until this moment, he'd never understood the remark made in frustrated jest. "Why do you hate me so much?" Richard asked.

Her stony expression didn't dissolve. "Once again, it has nothing to do with you. It's what Jenny wants, and at this time, I can give her very little. What I can give her, I shall. And right now, she wants to see no one. She wants privacy."

Marian sat down and began sorting papers on her desk. Richard realized that it was her way of dismissing him. However, he was in no mood to be brushed off. "If I could just talk to her, I know I could change her mind about allowing me to visit."

"Not at this time," Marian replied, with obvious patience. "It's nothing personal. It's a woman thing." She added the last remarks hesitantly, almost as if they might make amends for her harsh demeanor.

He struggled to sort out her meaning. "A 'woman thing'?" he asked slowly. "Are you saying she doesn't want me to see her because she looks bad?"

Marian gave him a sharp, penetrating look, but now that he had the opening, Richard barreled ahead with his argument. "I don't care how she looks. All I want to do is see her, hold her hand, and talk to her. I know I can make her feel better. I've always been able to take her mind off her troubles."

That much was true, Richard assured himself. That first summer, after her parents' deaths and after she'd come to live with Marian, he'd taken Jenny under his wing and showed her all his secret places to play on Martha's Vineyard. He'd taken her to the beach and shown her how to slip along a wall of seemingly solid granite to the narrow crevice that led to the cave. A cave full of pale blue light and shallow pools and mysteries from the sea. How he regretted not going there with her weeks before. Why had he lied about seeing some other girl? There was no one he wanted to be with more than Jenny.

Marian let out a deep sigh. "Richard, this discussion is getting us nowhere. You won't persuade me to go against Jenny's wishes. I will tell her how much you would like to come up to her hospital room, but I doubt it will change her mind."

"Can I at least talk to her on the phone?"

"Even taking phone calls would tax her, so she can't do that at this time."

"You're taking every opportunity away from me," Richard argued. "That's not right."

"I have no control over what is happening to Jenny," Marian insisted angrily. "Can you imagine how frustrating that is for me?"

Her candor surprised him. "I can imagine," he admitted.

"Then you understand that I'm not being deliberately heartless." He nodded. "Cancer is very cruel, Richard. What the doctors have to do to her to fight her cancer is very cruel. I know that her physical appearance is inconsequential to you, but for right now, how people think of her, and remember her, is most important to her."

"But—"

Marian held up her hand to stem his protest. "I can't take her illusions away from her. It would be callous of me."

It wasn't that Richard didn't understand—he did. Marian was simply protecting Jenny from Jenny's own fears. If only he could convince Jenny that he didn't care how she looked. "Do you think she'd read a letter from me if I wrote to her?"

"I think a letter would be ideal."

A letter was a poor substitute in Richard's mind, but perhaps he could use it to somehow persuade Jenny to allow him to be with her. As if she'd read his mind, Marian added, "Only don't make it a piece of propaganda—a tool for plying her with guilt in order for you to get your way."

"I'm not giving up."

"I don't expect you to. All I ask is that you be sensitive and try to see her perspective."

Richard clenched his jaw until it hurt to keep from saying anything he might regret. *It's not her fault*, he told himself. Trouble was, it was no one's fault, and so there was nothing he could do, no one he could blame. Richard whipped around, stomped across the thick pile carpet, and slammed out of the luxurious study.

Nine

FOR JENNY, THE days passed in a long unbroken chain of treatments and illness. The radiation treatments didn't hurt, but often made her nauseated, lethargic, and irritable. Her skin felt tight and sore. She was warned to stay out of sunlight without first applying sunscreen. Jenny found this advice laughable. She figured she'd never get out of the hospital, much less go to the beach again.

The combinations of potent drugs made her ravenous on some days, made it impossible for her to keep anything down on others. Sores formed in her mouth, and her beautiful long, black hair fell out in clumps. The cortisone medications gave her a "moonface," a peculiar plumpness that had her resembling a pumpkin. She felt so hideously ugly that she asked for all mirrors to be removed from her room.

Yet, for all the torture, Dr. Gallagher still couldn't achieve the goal of remission. Jenny began to think there was no such thing, that remission was simply a rumor, a carrot held out on a stick. "This form of leukemia is stubborn," Dr. Gallagher said. "Just hang on and keep the faith. We'll lick it."

Hang on. Jenny made his words her life's motto. But as the days passed, hanging on and keeping her faith that she'd overcome her disease became more difficult. The days she spent in isolation were bad enough, but the nights were impossible. She felt like a vampire, not only because of the frequent transfusions she received at night, but because she presumed herself to be a creature of the night, doomed to wakefulness, loneliness, cut off from all she knew and loved.

"Perhaps I could locate some of your classmates for you to talk to," her grandmother suggested.

Jenny recoiled in horror. Most of the girls in her prep school were boarders, and when each term ended, they went back home, or off to Europe, or away to family retreats. "There's no one I want to see," Jenny told her. "No one I want to see me like this."

Jenny's one joy was the letters she received from Richard. He wrote of his days on his job or of sailing out to Martha's Vineyard for the weekends.

I haven't gone once to our cave. I can't. Somehow, it's not right to go there without you. Remember the time you were eleven and stashed a supply of candy bars in a little hiding place in one of the rocks? And then when we were settled in telling ghost stories and you went to get them out, you found only empty wrappers because the crabs had gotten to them? You cried. I'm sorry I laughed at you. Okay—not real sorry—you looked sort of cute bawling over a

*bunch of shredded candy wrappers. I know I told
you that the ghost of some shipwrecked sailor had
probably gobbled them down. Of course, you pre-
tended to believe me. So now I want you to believe
something else I'm going to tell you. You will get
better and get out of the hospital! And when you
do, we'll go to the cave. We'll go sailing. We'll do
all the things we used to do.*

*Please believe me. And please change your mind
and let me come up for a visit. Your letters are
great, but nothing like seeing you in person.*

Seeing her in person was still the last thing Jenny
wanted Richard to do. It was more than vanity on
her part. It went beyond her not wanting him to see
her looking sick and ugly. She couldn't even explain
it to herself, but she knew that Richard represented
a world she might never know again. Just seeing
him, and facing completely the loss of that world of
beauty and innocence, of wellness and wholeness,
would be more than she could bear. *I'm a coward*,
she told herself, but it didn't make any difference.

One afternoon, when Mrs. Kelly was preparing to
return Jenny to her private room after a radiation
treatment, the nurse told her, "Men are working on
the private elevator today, so we'll have to take the
regular one. I hope you won't be too uncomfortable."

Jenny touched the scarf on her head, hoping it
was covering all of her bald head, and nodded nervously. She wasn't crazy about the way her grandmother and Mrs. Kelly treated her like a pampered
princess, but she didn't care much for mingling with
the healthy world either. "It'll be fine," Jenny said.

The public elevator was crowed with visitors,

nurses, orderlies, and technicians. Jenny felt self-conscious sitting in her wheelchair among them. Mrs. Kelly shielded the chair deftly to keep Jenny from being buffeted, but every time the door slid open, she caught glimpses of other floors, other areas of the hospital.

She recalled how large the hospital had seemed to her the first time she'd seen it, and realized that except for her room on a special floor, the chemo treatment room, the Radiation Department, and a few hallways, she'd never toured the inside of the place.

Again, the elevator door slid open, and someone from the hall yelled, "Hold the door, I'm coming!" The remaining people in the elevator waited patiently for the person who'd shouted, and Jenny gazed with interest out into the hallway. The walls were gaily painted with a circus theme, and the floor bustled with activity. A parade of kids of all shapes, sizes, and ages passed in front of the elevator door. Many of the children were bald, some were on crutches, others rolled their own wheelchairs.

Startled, Jenny stared out at them. She saw a girl who looked to be her age and could scarcely believe it. "Where are we?" she asked Mrs. Kelly.

"Pediatric oncology," Mrs. Kelly replied. "Remember, Boston Children's Hospital is one of the foremost treatment centers in the country, so many physicians send their patients here."

Intellectually, Jenny had known that, but now, seeing others, the message began to sink in. *They're just like me!* she thought. *We're all alike. We're all sick.*

The next morning, when her grandmother came to visit, Jenny told her about what she'd seen.

"Of course, my dear," Grandmother said with an

indulgent smile. "I made certain that you had the latest, newest technology available."

"But there looked to be so many others. I—I didn't think about it before now, but I'm not alone."

Grandmother looked puzzled. "Certainly you're not alone. You have Mrs. Kelly and me. Isn't one of us always here for you?"

How could her grandmother be missing the point? Jenny wondered. "How come I've never run into other kids during my treatments?"

"Because I've arranged for you to have total privacy." Jenny stared at her, dumbstruck. "That's what you wanted, isn't it? To be alone?"

Was it? Jenny asked herself. Was total isolation what she really wanted? "Maybe. Maybe not."

"Whatever you want, I'll try and get it for you." Grandmother tidied the bedcovers as she spoke.

"How about a rope ladder to the ground below?"

"It's good to see you feeling better." Grandmother smiled and kissed Jenny's forehead. "Can I get you something before I leave?"

Jenny said no, and once her grandmother had gone, she sent Mrs. Kelly on a wild-goose chase, climbed out of bed, and slipped on her embroidered cotton robe. Grateful that this was a day she didn't have a treatment and that she felt pretty good, Jenny scribbled a hasty note to Mrs. Kelly about going exploring and returning soon.

She took the repaired private elevator down to the ground floor, looked on a wall directory for the pediatric oncology floor, and took the public elevator there. *One good thing about being in my nightgown in a hospital*, Jenny told herself, *no one seems to notice how I'm dressed.*

When the elevator doors opened onto the children's cancer floor, Jenny stepped out into what seemed like another world. Murals of circus tents and painted ponies covered the walls. A tightrope walker looked real enough to touch.

"Are you all right?" The nurse's question made Jenny whip around.

"I'm fine." Her heart hammered. Would the nurse chase her away?

"Everyone's in the art therapy room. Don't you want to join them?"

"The what?"

"Art therapy classes," the nurse said with a sunny smile. "I hear they're making Christmas wreaths. Can you imagine? Christmas in July?"

She pointed toward a door, and Jenny hurried to it. Hesitantly, she swung it open and peeked inside. She saw kids, lots of kids, sitting at long tables heaped with mounds of pinecones, artificial greenery, ornaments, ribbons, paste, scissors, and glue. Christmas music was playing on a stereo, and several women were bent over, helping little hands shape wires into circles.

Jenny blinked, hardly believing her eyes. She felt like Dorothy viewing Munchkins for the first time. Had she gone over the rainbow and fallen into Oz? "Come in," a woman urged, when she saw Jenny at the door. "There's plenty of room at the teen table."

She pointed to a table of girls who sat working with a pile of materials. Yet, it wasn't the wreaths Jenny was seeing. She was looking at girls like herself. All were bald, but not concealing their baldness with scarves. One was missing an arm. Another's hand was attached to an IV line on a metal stand parked beside the table, and a third appeared incredibly thin and gaunt.

The girl with one arm saw Jenny and beckoned with her remaining hand. "Come on over and pull up a chair. We don't want to be having all this fun all by ourselves." She rolled her eyes, and the others giggled. "I'm Kimbra," she said. "Who are you, and when did you check in?"

Ten

"I'm Jenny." She pulled out a chair as she spoke.

"Welcome to Happy Hour," the girl with the IV said. "I'm Noreen, and this is Elaine. We had no idea there'd been a new admittance last night."

"Pay no attention to Noreen," Kimbra warned. "She considers herself the mouthpiece of the floor. If something's happening on Nine West, our chief reporter wants the scoop."

"You two look forward to every tidbit I collect, and you know it," Noreen insisted.

"If you're so good, why haven't you uncovered any information about the hospital's mystery guest?" Elaine asked with an innocent smile.

"A mystery guest?" Jenny asked, fascinated by the camaraderie between the three girls.

Noreen leaned closer to her. "There's someone famous up on one of the floors."

"There is?" Jenny leaned forward eagerly. "Who?"

Noreen glanced around. "We don't know, but I

think it's a movie star. Whoever it is has private times in the treatment rooms, and no one's allowed to mingle with him or her."

"You have an overactive imagination," Kimbra insisted.

"Famous people get cancer too," Noreen said defensively. "It *could* be someone superspecial."

"Or it could just be a superrich snob," Elaine offered.

Jenny was momentarily stunned into silence. They were talking about her! *She* was the mystery patient. She flushed, not wanting them to know, not wanting them to think she was someone who considered herself too good for them. "So what are we making here?" she asked, attempting to change the subject.

"Something dumb," Kimbra kidded. "But art therapy is one of our few diversions. We have it twice a week, so we go with the flow."

"What are we supposed to do?"

"I'll show you," Kimbra volunteered, and for the next thirty minutes, Jenny sorted through pinecones, ribbon, and decorative ornaments. Contentedly, she listened to the others chatter, asked a few questions, and answered vaguely when someone asked her something. She learned that she was the oldest of the four. Kimbra was fifteen and from a suburb of Baltimore. Elaine was fourteen and from rural Vermont. And Noreen was fifteen and from Quincy, a suburb of Boston.

"Noreen has ten brothers and sisters," Elaine told Jenny with admiration. "Out where I live, there's barely ten neighbors."

"You should try waiting in line for the bathroom at my house," Noreen joked. "That's why I'm the only one in this room who doesn't mind being in the hospital. I finally have some privacy."

"So, what are you in for?" Kimbra asked Jenny. "For me it's Ewing's sarcoma—that's bone cancer. They cut off my arm last year, and I had a lot of radiation. They thought they had it licked, but now it's turned up in my shoulder." With her remaining hand, she touched the shoulder of her amputated arm. "Radiation again. The pits."

Noreen said, "I've got non-Hodgkin's lymphoma in my stomach. That's a slow-growing tumor that's trying to take over my body."

"Yeah, like an alien," Elaine inserted.

"Cute." Noreen sniffed. "My doctor's trying to shrink it with X rays, then I'll have an operation to cut it out."

Jenny shuddered. At least Dr. Gallagher didn't have to cut up her insides.

"Leukemia," Elaine said. "This is my second time around. I got it when I was ten and had a really long remission. Then it popped up again."

Jenny found the news frightening. Although she realized that patients could relapse, she had been so focused on achieving her first remission, she hadn't thought beyond it. What if she relapsed too? "Leukemia for me too," she told the girls. "Just diagnosed." While it wasn't exactly the truth, Jenny didn't feel like fielding a bunch of embarrassing questions.

"Have you gotten a room assignment yet?" Noreen asked, as she pounded a hapless pinecone onto her wreath.

"Sort of."

Kimbra gave her a puzzled look, but before Jenny was forced to elaborate, Noreen piped up with, "So, why don't you ask your doctor to put you in with us?"

"Sure," Elaine agreed. "We have a room with four beds, and one's empty. The little girl who was using it went home Monday."

"You'd want me in your room?"

"Why not?" Kimbra said with a shrug. "We're about sick of each other's company, and the more the merrier."

"Sick of each other?" Elaine cried. "Just for that, I won't let you watch *General Hospital* this afternoon."

"And I refuse to fetch your basin if you have a puke attack after your afternoon treatment," Noreen added.

The one-armed Kimbra tossed a pinecone at the other two. They all laughed, and Jenny smiled reluctantly. Their sense of black humor, the way they kidded about their horrible illnesses, amazed her. Suddenly, the thought of going back up to her lonely, isolated room, with no one her age to talk with, became unbearable. "Let me tell my grandmother, before she makes other arrangements. Don't let anybody in that bed except me." Jenny flashed a bright smile as she stood. "I get first dibs."

"You want to move *where*?" Grandmother looked shocked as she asked Jenny this question.

"Down to the regular cancer floor," Jenny answered calmly, sitting up in her hospital bed that evening. "To share a room with three other girls."

"But why? You have everything you could possibly need or want right here."

"Everything except company." She held up her hand to head off her grandmother's protest. "Yes, you and Mrs. Kelly are very good to me, but when I met those girls this morning, I realized how much I've been missing. I've been totally cut off up here, Grandmother. Don't you understand?"

"I thought it was what you wanted. You still won't allow Richard to come visit."

"Richard's different. These girls are going through the same things I'm going through. They're sick and bald and taking treatments, and . . . well, we have cancer in common."

"But a *ward*, Jenny. Wards are so ordinary. Here, you have a private room, round-the-clock individual attention, anything you ask for. And what if you caught some kind of infection? You know that Dr. Gallagher told you chemo would lower your resistance."

"It's still a hospital, Grandmother. I'm sure they take precautions against germs." Jenny offered a chiding look. "Honestly, Grandmother, if I didn't know better, I'd say you were acting snobbish. That you didn't want me to mingle with these girls."

Marian's cheeks flushed. "I have nothing against the girls. Why, I don't even know them. It's simply that wards and sharing rooms are for people who can't afford better."

"And since I can, I should keep in my place and they in theirs. Is that what you're saying?"

"Not at all."

But Marian looked so flustered that Jenny reached out and covered her grandmother's hands with her own. "You've taken excellent care of me, and I love you very much. I wouldn't be asking this if it weren't important to me. More than important," she added hastily. "It's necessary. If I have to stay up here one more day, I'll go crazy."

"I've only wanted to protect you, Jenny. Don't you

know what I'd give to make all this go away for you?"

Jenny gazed at her levelly. "It's not going to go away. At least not by wishing. I've changed a lot these last two months. And I don't mean just on the outside." She smiled wryly. "All ,my life, I've been just a little bit different from my friends. I didn't grow up in a regular family with a mom and a dad. I was an orphan. I never boarded at school like all my friends. I was driven in a chauffeured car back and forth every day."

"I saw no need to ship you off to school. I wanted you with me."

"And I wanted to be with you. But things are different now. I may not even be able to return to school and my friends. I have to find my way through this thing that's happened to me by myself. I want to get well. I want to grow old and spend all that money you've socked away for me." Jenny squeezed her grandmother's hand. "And right now, I want to move in with Kimbra, Noreen, and Elaine. Please, don't disapprove."

Eleven

AFTER OBTAINING DR. Gallagher's approval, Jenny, Mrs. Kelly, and her grandmother moved her things down to the pediatric oncology ward early the next morning. Elaine was receiving a chemo treatment, and Noreen was in Radiology, so only Kimbra was present to help her settle in.

"Is this real silver?" Kimbra asked, holding up Jenny's antique fountain pen.

"Um—it was a gift."

"And this picture frame—was it a gift too? Wow, who's the hunk?" Kimbra held up a photograph of a smiling Richard standing on the bow of the *Triple H*. Jenny had been unable to force herself to send it home with her grandmother, so it remained with her, her only reminder of better days and of all the things she wanted to return to when remission was finally achieved.

"A friend," Jenny said.

"Just a friend?" Kimbra arched an eyebrow. Jenny

shot a sideways glance toward her grandmother. *Later*, she mouthed silently, and Kimbra caught the hint.

"We've scheduled a Monopoly marathon tonight in the activity room," Kimbra announced, setting down the photograph. "Want to join us?"

"What's that?"

"Once a week, we have an all-night game session. It helps take our minds off upchucking. If one of us gets too sick to play, then someone takes over her place at the board. We play until someone owns the board and the others are in bankruptcy." Kimbra grinned. "There's a certain sense of satisfaction that comes with winning, and showing opponents no mercy. The night nurses help out by offering us food—anything we want, anything we can keep down."

"You need your rest," Grandmother interjected.

Jenny had forgotten that Marian was eavesdropping. "I'm sure the nurses won't let us do anything that's harmful."

"Heck, no," Kimbra said. "They do their best to make us as happy as possible. They know how tough all this is on kids—especially little ones. Some nights, we all go down the hall and cuddle the younger kids. They get scared, and their mothers can't always stay round-the-clock."

Jenny had always liked little kids, although she'd never spent much time around them. And she vividly remembered what it felt like to be without the familiar comfort of her parents, to be alone and scared in a strange place. "It will be fun to do both things," Jenny replied. "I haven't played Monopoly in years." Not since one summer when it had rained almost every day. Then, she and Richard had set up a Monopoly game in her grandmother's sunroom and kept it going for weeks.

"Just don't get overtired," Grandmother warned.

Jenny insisted she could handle the schedule, then, feeling a certain amount of relief, said goodbye as her grandmother went home for the afternoon.

"She's awfully protective," Kimbra observed.

"She means well. I'm all she has."

"You're lucky to have family close by. Since my folks live in Baltimore, they can only get up here once or twice a month. And poor Elaine's folks can only make it every five or six weeks."

"How about Noreen's family? She lives in the city."

Kimbra grinned. "Every time you turn around, you're tripping over one of her kin. There's so many of them that I can't keep them all straight. She has a couple of older brothers who are really cute, but what guy's going to take a second look at a one-armed girl?"

"What guy's going to look seriously at any of us?" Jenny countered. "We're not exactly a bunch of beauty queens, you know."

Kimbra appraised Jenny carefully. "Sorry, Jenny, but not even baldness and a moonface can make you look ugly."

"You don't have to be kind—I'll share the dresser with you," Jenny quipped. Still, Kimbra's evaluation meant much to Jenny. She only wished she felt good enough about her looks to face Richard. She missed him. She wondered if he was dating anyone special now that he was alone in the city. *Don't torture your-*

self, she commanded silently. Nothing could have ever happened between them anyway.

"Are you still with me?"

Kimbra's question caused Jenny to start from her musings. "Absolutely."

"By the way you were staring into space, I thought you'd checked out."

"Only in my dreams," Jenny said with a sigh. "Only in my dreams."

Elaine returned from her chemo session looking white-faced and sick. "I won't throw up," Elaine mumbled. "I won't."

"Why do you fight it every time?" Noreen asked. Her radiation treatment hadn't wiped her out as much as Elaine's chemo one. "Just let it rip. You know you'll feel better."

Jenny understood completely. Vomiting was disgusting and very debilitating. "Would it help if I read to you?" she asked. "Kimbra says we don't start our Monopoly-a-thon until at least eleven."

"No one's read to me since I was a little kid."

"Sometimes it helps to concentrate on something other than how your insides feel," Jenny said. "And I have just the right book." She whipped out a dog-eared copy of *Gone with the Wind*. "I'll start with Scarlett flirting with all her boyfriends at the picnic at Twelve Oaks. That's where she meets Rhett, you know."

Jenny began to read, taking on different voices for the different characters. Soon, Kimbra and Noreen had gathered around Elaine's bed and were listening intently. She read until she was almost hoarse, but her suggestion worked. Elaine didn't throw up and finally drifted off to sleep. Jenny closed the book and went across the room to her bed.

"Good job," Noreen whispered.

"It really worked," Kimbra said.

"Sometimes it does." Jenny tossed the book down and stretched out on her bed. Suddenly, she was exhausted, then realized that she hadn't taken one nap that day, though lately she'd been taking several out of boredom. "Tomorrow is my turn down in the chamber of horrors," she said with a sigh.

"So we'll read to you," Kimbra promised.

"With three of us on chemo, what happens when we finish the book?" Noreen wanted to know.

"Don't worry." Jenny pulled open her bedside drawer and pulled out several thick paperback novels. "*The Fountainhead, Anna Karenina,* and *War and Peace.* I think we can manage to fill up the hours."

The two girls laughed, and Jenny smiled too. How good it was to hear the sound of laughter. How good it felt not to be alone in the room. Why hadn't she discovered these friends before now?

Richard confronted Marian in her parlor one evening after he left work. "Why isn't she getting better? Why is it taking so long?"

Marian rubbed her temples with her fingertips. "Dr. Gallagher *is* concerned that it's taking an inordinately long time for Jenny to achieve a remission."

"Isn't there anything else he can do?"

"Unfortunately, no. He's told me about bone marrow transplants, but they're still rather experimental."

"I've never heard of them."

"It's a new frontier, the new hope for leukemia treatment. They actually transplant bone marrow from a healthy donor into a leukemia victim. It's had some success when the transplant has been between identical twins."

Richard's heart sank. Jenny wasn't a twin. "Well, I know that she and I aren't related, but I'll be a donor if they can use me."

Marian considered him kindly. "Medical science hasn't solved the rejection problem yet. According to Dr. Gallagher, each person's immune system is unique, and when a foreign substance enters the bloodstream, the body begins to fight it off. In order for a transplant to work, they have to destroy a person's immune system, and that makes a person susceptible to any germ that comes along."

"So even when good marrow could cure Jenny, her body won't accept it. Some hope," he added sarcastically. "Is this the best that can be done for her? All the chemo and radiation?"

"I've contacted doctors all over the world, even clinics specializing in cancer research. They tell me the same thing. For now, this is all that can be done for Jenny. In ten years—in 1988 instead of 1978, more advances will probably change the situation for patients."

"Born too soon" Richard said, feeling defeated. "What a paradox." He remembered the night of the dance. If only he could put his arms around her again, he wouldn't let go. "She writes that she likes the ward she's in."

"At first, I didn't approve," Marian admitted, "but the other girls have been good for her morale. According to Dr. Gallagher, a positive mental outlook is helpful."

Richard wished his morale were better. It had been too long since he'd seen Jenny, and he missed her. In another month, he'd be returning to Princeton, and although he wasn't looking forward to it, he had to admit that attending classes would beat his summer job by a long shot. And beat the waiting for Jenny to come home. The endless waiting.

Twelve

DR. GALLAGHER PUT Jenny on a new experimental drug that left her so vulnerable to secondary infections, she had to wear a mask over her nose and mouth that filtered out germs from the air. The drug made her sick, she dropped six pounds in a week, but her blood work began to show improvement. Fewer leukemia cells—*blasts*—showed up in her bone marrow.

"After two weeks, we'll take you off this stuff and put you back on more conventional therapy," Dr. Gallagher told her. "So keep the faith." He used his familiar words of encouragement and squeezed her hand.

At the same time Jenny was being pumped full of the potent new chemical, Noreen's doctor scheduled her for surgery to remove the tumor in her stomach. The night before she was to be taken down for the operation, the four roommates huddled together in their room. "I hope this guy knows what he's doing and doesn't take out my whole stomach," Noreen grumbled.

Jenny could tell Noreen was trying to keep up a brave front for them as well as her family, who had just left amid promises to be back at the crack of dawn.

"Think of the bright side," Elaine offered. "You would never have to worry about dieting again."

"Plus, what they're taking out of you won't show up on your outside," Kimbra said, waving her stump of an arm. "That should count for something."

Noreen pulled her covers up to her chin. "Do you have any books to take my mind off tomorrow, Jenny?"

"All I can think of is some of the psalms in the Bible."

Noreen made the sign of the cross. "Ma told me our parish priest is coming with them tomorrow to wait through my surgery. I guess if things don't go right, he can give me last rites."

"Stop talking like that," Jenny's voice sounded muffled because of the mask, but her tone was sharp enough to make Noreen look startled. "You're going to come through this just fine. In fact, after it's all over and you're back down here with us, I'll throw you a party."

Noreen perked up. "What kind of party?"

"What kind do you want?"

"Something with a gigantic cake. And ice cream."

"You'll have a vat of the stuff."

"And a rock band."

"The loudest."

"Can I have my brothers and sisters come too? And some of my old friends from school and the neighborhood?"

Just then, the medications nurse, Mrs. Henry, entered the room carrying a tray of assorted pills and cups of liquid medicines. "Teatime," she announced. Then, glancing at their faces, she asked, "What are you four cooking up?"

"Us? Why nothing," Kimbra replied innocently.

"Then why do you all look as if you're up to something?"

"Jenny's going to throw me a party after my surgery," Noreen explained. "Something small and private."

Nurse Henry still looked suspicious. "Since when have any of you done anything small and private? I mean, who started the war during last week's art therapy session?"

"Oh, that." Jenny said, recalling how during the session, Noreen and Kimbra had decided to decorate each other, in addition to their crafts projects, with gold and silver glitter. Soon, the entire room had erupted into chaos, and glitter had fallen like rain.

"Yes, that." The nurse tried to keep a straight face. "I hear that the janitors are still picking glitter out of the carpet."

"I'm still finding it embedded in my head," Elaine said, rubbing the top of her bald head with her hand.

"And you expect me to believe that you're going to have a sedate little party?"

All of the girls exchanged glances. "Let's just say it won't be boring," Jenny replied.

"Well, I think all of you should take your medicine and turn out the lights. Noreen has a big day ahead of her tomorrow."

"I'd almost forgotten. Why did you have to remind me?"

"Will you make sure someone keeps us informed, since we can't go into the recovery room and check on her ourselves?" Elaine asked.

"Someone will keep you posted," the nurse assured them.

"We have to stick together," Kimbra told her. "We *are* the Four Musketeers, you know."

"More like the Four Horsemen of the Apocalypse," Mrs. Henry said with a wry smile.

After she left, Elaine turned to the others. "Who are the Four Horsemen of the whatever-she-said?"

"I've heard of them," Noreen replied. "They're in the Bible."

"I think they're associated with major calamities," Jenny said. "Like pestilence and famine."

"Who mentioned famine?" Elaine asked. "I'm so hungry, I could eat the paint off the walls."

"You're *always* hungry," Kimbra insisted.

"How can you talk about food when I'm about to have my stomach amputated? Give me a break!"

"You're not thinking about the bright side—diets will be a thing of the past," Jenny told her returning to what Elaine had said earlier.

Noreen let out an exasperated screech, which started them giggling. An hour later, they turned off the lights for the night, but lay in the darkness and talked until one by one, they fell asleep.

Jenny felt as if she'd scarcely closed her eyes when she heard the orderlies come to take Noreen down for surgery. In the semidarkness of the room, Jenny was instantly awake. "Keep the faith," she told Noreen. "Make sure that surgeon gets all the bad stuff."

Jenny knew her friend had been given preop medication, which would make her groggy. As she was rolled past on the gurney, Noreen held up her thumb and offered a lopsided smile. Jenny felt her heart clutch. *"Be all right,"* she whispered to the darkness after Noreen had been wheeled from the room.

Neither she, Kimbra, nor Elaine felt like doing anything that morning. They lounged around their room, reading and watching TV. Outside, it poured rain, the weather matching their glum moods.

"I would have won ten thousand dollars if I'd been on that game show," Elaine said halfheartedly during a particular program. "Maybe someday, I'll go on one, and they'll have a category on cancer. I'm sure I could answer every question."

"What would you do with ten thousand dollars if you won it?" Jenny asked.

"She'd probably fritter it away on hamburgers," Kimbra answered for Elaine.

"A lot you know," Elaine said with toss of her head. "I'd save it and go to college."

College. The word pricked Jenny. Naturally, college had been in her plans. Her grandmother had spoken often about Wellesley as a fine place for "proper young women." At the moment, Jenny couldn't remember the last time she'd thought about school, much less college.

"Why is it taking so long?" Kimbra blurted, irritated. "They should have finished by now."

"Maybe her doctor's just slow," Jenny offered.

"This whole place is slow. We all should have been out of here ages ago."

"I wish—" Elaine began.

"Well, stop wishing," Kimbra snapped. "Wishing

for something is dumb and stupid. Wishes don't ever come true, so why bother?"

Jenny felt sorry for Elaine, who seemed more optimistic about life overall, but she certainly understood where Kimbra was coming from. Girls their age with cancer had to be practical. Pollyanna thinking led nowhere.

As the day dragged on, their collective mood grew more gloomy. It was almost suppertime when Shannon, one of Noreen's older, married sisters came into their room. She looked haggard and red-eyed from crying.

"What's wrong?" Kimbra jumped from her bed and rushed over to Shannon. "How's Noreen?"

"She's out of surgery and in the recovery room," Shannon said with a quivery voice.

Jenny sagged with relief. "But that's great news," she said.

"Yes and no." Shannon wiped her eyes on a wadded tissue.

"Explain." Kimbra used her best no-nonsense voice.

"Before her surgery, Noreen made me promise to come and tell you three everything."

"What's everything?" Elaine wanted to know. "Didn't they get all her tumor?"

That possibility hadn't crossed Jenny's mind. She had assumed that once the doctors operated, Noreen's stomach tumor would be a thing of the past.

"Not exactly." Shannon blew her nose. "Her doctor told us that when he opened her up, he found other tumors. Many others. In fact, there were so many that he couldn't begin to get them all. So, he took out the largest ones, then sewed her back up. As soon as Noreen recuperates from the surgery, they're going to send her home. You see, there's nothing else they can do for her. Nothing. My sister's going to die."

Thirteen

"NOREEN'S DYING!" JENNY sobbed to her grandmother that evening when she came for a visit. "Noreen's just fifteen! She's younger than me."

"I'm so sorry, Jenny." Grandmother stroked Jenny's back, attempting to calm her.

"It's wrong! Why is this happening to her? Why can't the doctors *do* something to save her? Why did they put her through all the torture of chemo and radiation if it wasn't going to make her well?"

"They had no way of knowing, Jenny. They had to *try*."

"Try! I'm sick of hearing *try*. Why can't they make her well?"

"You're getting yourself all worked up over something you can't change. It isn't healthy."

"Nothing's healthy, is it? And I don't care if I'm all worked up. . . . I want to change things for Noreen. I want to make things different for all of us."

Grandmother looked distraught, and Jenny realized that her anger was only upsetting the woman. She wanted to stop her tirade, but couldn't. It was as if her frustration had reached volcanic proportions and she was helpless to control the eruption. In despair, Jenny buried her face in her hands and wept bitterly.

Her grandmother stroked her tenderly. "I wish I could change all of this for you, Jenny. I wish I could make it all go away with a wave of my hand, but of course, I can't. Sometimes, I weigh all of what's happening to you ... to us ... against other calamities that have occurred in my life. I remember the day your father and I had our disagreement."

Jenny's sobs quieted as she listened. Grandmother rarely talked about her son—Jenny's father.

"Warren had spent the summer in London and had come home on fire with idealistic dreams about changing the world. He'd also met your mother and fallen in love with her. I refused to listen to him, refused to believe that he could want anything other than the plans I had made for him. We had a terrible fight."

Jenny looked up, wiping her cheeks with the hem of the bed sheet. Her grandmother's eyes had taken on a faraway look.

"He stormed out of the house and returned to London. In reality, he stormed out of my life. Do you know, we didn't speak again until you were born?"

Jenny shook her head. "They never told me."

"You were the magnet that brought us back together." Grandmother smiled wistfully. "It was a tentative union, but at least, we were on speaking terms. He and your mother, Barbara, came for a visit when you were only three months old. I was prepared to dislike her and be indifferent to you." Another smile. "Instead, I discovered a lovely young woman who adored my son and their child, and the most beautiful baby girl I'd ever set eyes upon."

"I didn't know," Jenny said.

"When they returned to London and got an assignment with the Peace Corps in Africa, I was heartbroken. Even then, I assumed your father wanted to return to my world. He did not, of course. He had his own world. And when he died, my world changed forever."

"You inherited me."

"Yes. . . . Barbara had no family to speak of in Britain, so you came to me. You were a frightened child, all alone in the world. I was terrified about raising you."

"You were?" Jenny never thought her grandmother was afraid of anything. She always seemed so confident, so in control.

"I hadn't been around a child in years, and suddenly, I was responsible for my granddaughter."

"I don't remember much about that time. I only remember being scared." She remembered Richard and the day of her parents' funeral, when he'd taken her hand. From that moment, she had begun to adore him. "Everything here was so different. The weather was cold, and I couldn't run around outside and play. And I missed my parents."

Grandmother traded Jenny a wad of clean tissues for the soaked hem of the sheet. "Certainly not what either of us planned for, was it?" Jenny shook her head. "But after having you with me for a month, I realized how empty, how hollow my life had been until you came into it."

"I remember running through your living room

and breaking your good vase. I thought you would send me back to Africa."

"The vase meant nothing, Jenny. By then, I had learned that the only thing that counts in this life is relationships. I had learned that the plans we make for our lives can't always be fulfilled, but that sometimes the change is extraordinarily wonderful.

"And over the years, I've realized that something good can come out of the darkest moments of life if we simply wait out the darkness." She arched an eyebrow and added, "Not that I like having my will thwarted, you understand."

Jenny managed a smile. "Are you telling me you're stubborn?"

"I call it Yankee determination."

Jenny toyed with the wad of tissue. "What good can come out of this, Grandmother? I want to believe what you're telling me, but I can't see what good can come from Noreen's dying at fifteen and my being sick with leukemia."

"I don't know either," Grandmother admitted. "But for some reason, some of us are asked to walk more difficult paths than others."

New tears formed in Jenny's eyes as she said, "Well, this path is really hard, and right now, I can't see any reason for it. And I'm sure I never will."

That night, Jenny lay awake in the dark. She envied Elaine and Kimbra, who were asleep under their covers, but for her, sleep was impossible. She knew she could ring for a nurse and get a pill to help her sleep, but she didn't want that either. With a sigh, she tossed off the covers, slipped on her robe, and padded down the dimly lit hall looking for someone to talk to.

She passed by one of the children's rooms and heard a soft whimper. She went inside and discovered a small girl huddled in her bed and crying. "Can I help?" Jenny asked, leaning down and whispering.

The little girl's eyes grew wide with fright. "Are you going to give me a shot?"

"Why, no."

"Are you a doctor?"

"No . . . I heard you crying, that's all."

Still, the girl looked skeptical. "Why's that thing on your face? Is something wrong with your mouth?"

Jenny touched the mask. It had become so much a part of her that she'd forgotten she was wearing it. "Nope. I have a very *big* mouth. See?" She slipped off the mask and opened wide, causing the girl to sniff and smile. "I'm really a mermaid, and sometimes, I have trouble breathing real air."

The girl giggled. "Mermaids have fish tails. Where's your fish tail?"

Jenny glanced down. "Oops. I must have lost it." She ducked down and looked under the child's bed. "It's not there. Hum-m-m. Wonder where I left it? That thing is so hard to keep track of. . . ."

The girl giggled again. "You're teasing me."

"Yes, I am." Jenny pulled a chair next to the bed. "I'm Jenny. What's your name?"

"Betsy. I'm six." She held up six fingers.

"I'm sixteen."

"I get lots of shots," Betsy said. "I hate shots. They're making me take medicine too, and it tastes bad. I hate it here. I want to go home."

"Me too."

"My mom couldn't stay with me because she's going to have a baby. I miss her."

Jenny's heart twisted. She imagined how torn Betsy's mother must feel, having to leave her child alone to face the terrors of the night because of her pregnancy. She touched Betsy's soft blond curls. Jenny knew that soon the silken locks would fall out in handfuls and Betsy would be bald and ill from chemo. *Another victim*, she thought. "How would you like me to read you a story?" Jenny asked.

"Will you?" Betsy looked so eager that Jenny smiled broadly. "I have some books." Betsy fumbled under her covers and extracted several worn copies of books by Dr. Seuss. She handed them to Jenny and settled back against her pillow. "I can read them by myself," she said, "but it's better when someone reads them to me."

Glad to find a way to help pass the seemingly endless night, Jenny took the books and began to read.

By midmorning the next day, Jenny couldn't pull herself out of bed. Her throat felt scratchy, and her head ached. "How's Noreen?" she asked Kimbra, shielding her eyes from the sunlight streaming in the window. Her eyes felt sore in their sockets.

"Still recuperating."

"Does she know about her other tumors?"

"I don't think so. Are you all right?" Kimbra peered closely at Jenny's face.

"I'm hot all over."

"I'll get a nurse."

"No . . . don't . . ."

But Kimbra was gone before the words were half formed. She returned with a nurse, who shook down a thermometer and placed it under Jenny's tongue. A minute later, she pulled it out, read it, then hurried from the room.

Fourteen

Jᴇɴɴʏ ꜰᴇʟᴛ ᴀꜱ if she were burning up. Her chest felt
tight, her arms and legs like lead weights. The cool
hands of the nurses were the only thing that comforted her. Dr. Gallagher arrived quickly, listened to
her lungs through his stethoscope, then ordered her
to be taken down to Radiology for lung X rays. He
wore a mask, yet Jenny saw the serious look in his
eyes.

She wanted to make a joke, but it took too much
effort to form words, so she simply closed her eyes.
Voices drifted in and out of her hearing. She heard
Kimbra say, "But she was fine last night at bedtime."
She heard a teary Elaine say, "First Noreen, now
Jenny. She has to be all right, Kimbra. She *has* to!"

Jenny heard her grandmother speaking to her and
felt her cool dry hand against her forehead. She
struggled to open her eyes and tell her not to worry,
but couldn't. Eventually, Jenny heard snatches of
conversation between Dr. Gallagher and her grand-

mother: ". . . pneumonia . . . infection . . . very ill . . . isolation . . . intensive care . . ."

At one point, Dr. Gallagher leaned over and said, "Jenny, you're going on a little ride down to ICU, where you can get round-the-clock nursing. Don't be alarmed, but I'm going to put you on a respirator for a while, just until your lungs clear up. It will help you breathe easier, so relax . . . we're going to fix you up."

A machine that could breathe . . . Jenny thought the information fascinating. She understood they were going to move her out of her room, and she tried to ask them not to, tried to ask Kimbra and Elaine not to let anybody take her place in the room. But again, she found talking much too difficult.

Hands lifted her onto a gurney, and she felt the motion of being rolled down the hall. Bright lights flashed past overhead. She floated, as if on the sea, and she embraced the sensation. She imagined that she was on the ocean, adrift on billowing waves of deep cobalt blue. She imagined that Richard was with her, holding her hand and smiling, his green eyes as bright as emeralds.

Suddenly, she wanted to see him again. She wanted to touch him, have him hold her as he had the night they danced at the country club. Why had she acted so stubborn these past weeks? Why had she refused to let him visit her? She'd been stupid. *Richard.* She cried out his name in her heart.

Hands settled her on a bed. Needles pricked her arms, tubing lay against her skin. She heard the unfriendly hiss of machines all around her, the rattle of bed rails being raised, fencing her in.

A crushing heaviness seized her chest, and she gasped for air. *What if I die and never see him again?*

Tears slid from the corners of her eyes. She felt helpless, hopeless, alone. She heard one nurse tell another, "Poor kid. She's crying."

She heard the other say, "Impossible. She's not even conscious."

She felt dizzy and saw what seemed like a dark hole reaching out for her. Subconsciously, she backpedaled, but the hole grew larger, until she had no choice but to fall into it . . . down . . . down . . . like Alice down the rabbit-hole.

In the ICU waiting room, Richard paced the floor as a caged animal caught in a trap. Marian sat in a chair, her back stiff and straight, her thin, veined hands clasped in her lap. *Ten minutes.* That's all anyone was allowed to go into ICU every hour. *Every other hour for me*, he reminded himself.

On the day he'd learned of Jenny's setback, he'd gone straight to Marian and begged to be allowed to see her. "I—I don't know," Marian had said. "I'm not sure it's what Jenny would want."

He could tell Marian was genuinely torn, and he used her ambivalence to his advantage. "She'll never know," he replied. "It'll be our secret. But I have to see her. It isn't right not to let me, and you know it."

In the end, Marian had agreed. Now, ten days later, there was little change in Jenny's condition, even though she'd been placed on a respirator and pumped full of antibiotics to fight off the persistent infection.

"Ironic, isn't it?" Marian's question stopped Richard's restless pacing. "For the first time since her diagnosis, Jenny was free of leukemic cells. They were going to let her go home and continue her treatment as an outpatient. And then this happened. An ordinary germ has knocked her out."

Richard saw permanent lines of worry etched in Marian's face. She looked to have aged ten years over the past three months. "She'll get well," he insisted. "She can't have been freed of cancer only to go down to pneumonia."

"I hope you're correct."

Richard glanced at his watch and saw that it was time for his visit to ICU. "I'll be back," he told Marian, who only nodded and continued to stare into space.

He entered the glass-walled chamber where Jenny lay surrounded by the tools of technology. A tube, attached to a respirator, protruded from her throat where the doctor had cut a hole in her trachea and inserted it. Wires snaked from her chest and hooked up to a monitor that kept a constant vigil over her heartbeat.

She looked as if she were asleep. Her face was gaunt, but even so, he could see her beauty through the ashen skin stretched tight over delicate facial bones. Dark circles smudged her eyes, and a fine fuzz of hair had begun to grow on her scalp. Tentatively, he reached out and touched the new growth. It felt as soft as down.

A knot filled his throat, and he could scarcely swallow around it. Rage filled him, blinding, white-hot anger that wanted to make him explode. Why was this happening to her? Was there no one to help her? Rationally, he knew the doctors were doing everything possible, but he sensed in his gut that her life didn't lie in the hands of medicine.

In the glare of the artificial lights, the walls of the cubicle seemed to fade away. And he saw Jenny through the eyes of memory, on the Easter Sunday of the previous year, when she'd been fifteen. She was dressed in wispy voile the color of buttercups. She wore a straw hat, and her long, dark hair hung in loose waves down her back.

When he'd seen her sitting in the pew, when she'd turned and caught his eye and smiled, his breath had almost stopped. It was if he were seeing her for the first time. She wasn't the kid he'd grown up with, taught to sail, run with, barefoot, on the beaches. She was suddenly different, more beautiful than any girl he knew at college. Maybe that was when his feelings toward her began to change. Perhaps that was when he began to love her, and to want her in every way.

Richard shook his head, dislodging the shimmering picture. *"You can't die, Jenny,"* he whispered. She had so much to live for. *They* had so much to live for. He felt a firm resolve grab hold of him as he realized what he knew he must do. He would become a lawyer the way his father wanted. He would work hard, earn money, become the kind of man Marian would allow Jenny to marry. Suddenly, his future looked full of purpose and direction.

But first, she had to get well. And only God could grant that wish. He closed his eyes and rocked back on his heels. If he was going to be an attorney, and if God was the final judge, then, at this moment, he had an opportunity to plead his first case.

He ignored the incessant noise of the machines and bowed his head. *Dear God . . . help her . . . please . . .* Richard swallowed, feeling inadequate with words of prayer and petition. He prayed the simple words again and again, until a nurse came to remind that his time in ICU was long since up.

Richard cleared his throat, bent, and kissed Jenny's forehead, hoping with all that was in him that God had heard him and would be lenient. Jenny was all he wanted. Hope for a future with her was all he had.

Fifteen

~⌒⊱⌒~

RICHARD WAS SITTING alone in the waiting room when a one-armed girl wearing a bathrobe entered. Self-consciously, she stopped in her tracks and clutched her robe tightly across her breasts with her remaining hand. "I—I thought Mrs. Crawford would be in here," she said.

"She's in with Jenny," Richard replied. "Ten minutes doesn't last very long, so feel free to sit down and wait."

The girl hesitated, but then crossed to the other side of the small room and eased into a chair. "How's Jenny doing?" she asked.

"No change." Richard fiddled with a Styrofoam coffee cup. "You a friend of hers?" He recalled Jenny's writing to him about a girl who'd lost an arm to cancer.

"I'm Kimbra Bradley, one of Jenny's roommates. I knew I couldn't get in to see her, but the nurses in ICU know how worried we are about Jenny, so sometimes they let me stand outside the glass partition and look in at her." Kimbra sighed helplessly. "I know there's nothing I can do for her, but I couldn't sleep tonight, and so I came up just to hang around. You don't mind, do you?"

"I don't mind."

Richard stared at the floor, trying not to let his eyes wander to Kimbra and the empty sleeve of her robe. When he'd been in high school, he'd seen Vietnam vets in an antiwar demonstration. Every one of the protestors had been maimed and was missing an arm, a leg, a hand, or a foot. He could still recall his internal horrified reaction to them. Even now, he wondered what it would be like to go through life handicapped in such a way.

"You're Richard, aren't you?"

"How did you know?" Uncomfortable as he felt around the girl, he was glad to have some company.

"Jenny keeps your picture next to her bed."

"She does?"

"Sometimes, she just lies in bed staring at it. I've told her she should let you come up for a visit. I know your visit would do wonders for the morale of her friends."

"What do you mean?"

"We don't see many good-looking guys on the oncology floor," Kimbra explained with a grin.

Richard returned her smile. "I wouldn't be seeing her now, except that I begged her grandmother. You won't tell Jenny, will you?"

"Not if you don't want me to."

"I don't want to upset her." He stretched his long legs out in front of him. "I could never figure why she was so set against my seeing her in the first place. I understand how bad her treatments are, but that's no reason for her to keep me away."

"You know us girls—it matters to us what we look like."

"Jenny's never made a big deal over her looks before. It doesn't seem like her to care about it now."

"It's not vanity," Kimbra explained. "Jenny's not conceited. It's more than that. . . . It's a way a person has of protecting herself, of keeping control of some little area of her life because she doesn't have control of anything else. I wish I could describe it better." Kimbra shrugged, making the empty sleeve on her robe bob and swing.

Against his will, Richard's gaze followed the dangling sleeve. Kimbra's gaze followed his. "It's all right," she told him when he quickly glanced away. "I'm used to people's reactions."

"I'm sorry," he said sincerely.

"My doctor was afraid my cancer was coming back into my shoulder, so I'm going through lots of radiation treatments."

"Are the treatments helping?"

"I think so." She grinned again. "I hope so. Although this has kind of put a cramp in my basketball career. Do you suppose they give sports scholarships for tiddlywinks? I can play that with one arm."

"I'll check for you when I get back to Princeton," he joked.

"I'm hoping to get out of here before school starts." She looked toward the doorway. "I know poor Jenny won't be able to start school on time even if she gets out of ICU tomorrow. She'll need time to recuperate."

He hadn't thought about school for Jenny. How would she handle attending classes?

"How about you?" Kimbra asked. "You must be going back to campus soon too."

"Classes start in a few weeks. I'll be a junior, but even after I graduate, I'll have four years of law school to face." Restless, Richard shifted forward in his chair. Marian had been gone a lot longer than ten minutes. "Do you suppose everything's all right?" he asked.

At that moment, Marian swept into the room, and she was smiling. "Jenny opened her eyes," Marian exclaimed. "She opened them and looked right at me. The nurse has called Dr. Gallagher, and he's on his way to the hospital. I think the worst is over, Richard. I think she's beaten her pneumonia."

Richard leapt up, feeling such relief that tears misted his eyes. "Maybe I could take one last look at her before she wakes up all the way and knows I'm there," he said.

Marian nodded vigorously, her haggard expression replaced by one of elation. Kimbra also stood, saying, "I'm going to go wake up Elaine and tell her. We'll celebrate and plan something special for when Jenny comes back to the room." But Richard was already out the door and into ICU before Kimbra finished her comment.

In the glass cubicle, Jenny looked no different to him, but when he touched her cheek, she stirred. He felt torn. He didn't want her to wake and see him. Still, he couldn't go away and leave her either. He promised himself that when all this was over, he'd move heaven and earth to be with her.

Richard bent and brushed his lips over hers, hoping that somehow, his kiss might magically communicate his love for her. That his touch might somehow bring her back to him.

Jenny felt as if she were fighting against the ocean's undertow. The sensation was one of struggling valiantly toward the shoreline only to be sucked backward by a strong ocean current she was too weak to fight. Just when she was certain she would drown, a wave of mammoth size lifted her and spit her onto the beach. Her eyelids fluttered open, and she expected to see sand and seaweed and to taste salt. Instead, she saw Dr. Gallagher bending over her and tasted panic.

"Welcome back," he said, a relieved smile splitting his face.

She tried to talk, but her throat was so sore, she could barely swallow.

Dr. Gallagher said, "Take it easy. I just pulled your trach tube, so your throat will hurt for a few days. You gave us quite a scare, Jenny, but you came through. All you need now is rest to get your strength back," She turned pleading eyes on him, and he smiled again. "You want to know when you can get out of here, don't you?"

She nodded.

"A few more days, then I'll send you back to your room. Right now, your grandmother wants to see you, and you know how difficult it is to keep her at bay."

Jenny attempted a smile, but the effort hurt.

"I'll send her in," Dr. Gallagher said, "and I'll check on you in a few hours." He held up his thumb. "Keep the faith," he added, stepping away from her bed.

Jenny closed her eyes and listened to the beep of

the heart monitor machine. *It's good to be back,* she told herself, although she had no earthly idea where she'd been.

Over the next two days, Jenny continued to recover, but she felt weak and listless. She barely had the strength to sit propped up with pillows. The nurses spoon-fed her weak broth, and slowly, the burning sensation in her throat eased. A large piece of white gauze covered sutures on her neck, and deep bruises across the backs of her hands and the insides of her elbows reminded her of what she'd been through.

"Your veins kept collapsing, and they had to hunt for new ones for your IVs," her grandmother explained, stroking her bruised skin. "The bruises will heal."

"What did they use—an ice pick?" Jenny asked, her voice sounding hoarse.

Grandmother chuckled. "Nice to hear your sense of humor's still intact."

"How are my friends? What about Noreen?"

"She's been sent home," Grandmother said. "Now, save your energy. We'll talk more later."

On her third day of recovery in ICU, Jenny heard a commotion outside her glass wall. She raised herself up and saw one of the nurses leading Kimbra, Elaine, Betsy, and two other girls she recognized from her floor. The group was dressed in bathrobes and holding large squares of white paper.

They marched single file and stopped in front of her enclosure, peered in at her with big smiles, then held up the papers, pressing them against the glass. Each paper held a painted block letter. H-E-L-L-O was what the message was to have read, except that little Betsy, who was holding the O, had somehow gotten ahead of Kimbra, who held the H.

The message read: O-H-E-L-L. Jenny blinked. Kimbra glanced down, rolled her eyes in exasperation, and shuffled Betsy down to the end of the line. *OHELL.* Kimbra offered a helpless shrug, but Jenny caught her eye, and for the first time in weeks, Jenny laughed aloud.

Sixteen

❦

"I'M GOING TO miss you all. Promise you'll write me." Elaine spoke as she packed her small suitcase.

"Of course, we'll write," Kimbra said. "We can't break up the old gang, can we, Jen?"

Jenny murmured her agreement, but she did have mixed emotions. She hadn't been back in her room for twenty-four hours when Elaine had been released to return home, her second remission accomplished. Jenny was glad for Elaine, but envious. She longed to go home.

"What about your outpatient treatments?" Jenny asked. "Vermont's a long way to commute."

"No need for me to. Dr. Gallagher's sending my chemo protocols up to my local hospital."

"Then who knows when we'll see you," Kimbra grumbled.

"You're leaving too," Elaine reminded Kimbra.

Jenny felt another twinge of jealousy. Kimbra was

headed home also. That meant Jenny would be the only one left in the room.

"But I live closer to Boston."

"Why don't you both come visit me over the Christmas holidays?" Jenny asked impulsively. "Do you think your folks will let you?"

"Maybe. It sure would be something to look forward to." Elaine sat atop her bulging suitcase and snapped the locks. "How about Noreen? Do you think she'll be able to join us?"

Jenny glanced over at Kimbra, who sighed. "Who knows? The last time I called, her mother said she was sick. I don't think she's doing very well."

An uncomfortable silence filled the room. Jenny understood what no one wanted to say out loud—by the holidays, Noreen could be too sick to leave the house. "Well, we'll all keep in touch for sure. It's only three months until Christmas."

"How about you, Jenny? When are you blowing this joint?"

"Dr. Gallagher says that my blood work looks good, but that he wants to make certain I can fight off any other infection before he releases me."

"I'm sure it won't be much longer," Elaine replied. "Now that you're in remission, they'll get you out of here as soon as possible."

"Not soon enough," Jenny said. She felt as if the pneumonia setback had stalled her life and she couldn't get it moving again.

"Can you believe I'm actually looking forward to getting back to school?" Elaine exclaimed.

"Me too." Kimbra flopped into a nearby chair. "Anything beats lying around this place."

Jenny knew she wouldn't be returning to school for the start of the term. When she'd mentioned it, her grandmother had said, "I would never allow you to leave the house so soon. I'll hire you a tutor to keep you on grade level."

"But I don't want to lie around doing nothing," Jenny had cried.

"Going to school with so many possibilities of your getting sick again is out of the question. You'll have a private tutor. You'll keep up with your classmates, but there's no sense in taking foolish chances with your health."

Jenny had appealed to Dr. Gallagher, but surprisingly, he endorsed her grandmother's plans. "Wait until after the first of the year," he told her. "After you complete your outpatient therapy. You'll be stronger, and we'll have a better idea as to the course of your illness."

She started to argue, but realized it would be futile. Perhaps they were right. Maybe by the beginning of January, she'd be completely recovered. Her hair would have had time to grow out, and by then, maybe she wouldn't look like such a freak. Resigned to having her life once again manipulated by cancer, Jenny told herself to be patient and wait out her recovery without complaining.

Elaine left that afternoon amid hugs and tears. Kimbra returned home two days later. "Don't forget me!" Jenny begged Kimbra while her parents were packing her things and checking her out.

Kimbra gave Jenny a one-arm hug. "What are you going to do about Richard?" Kimbra asked, pulling away and motioning toward the photo of Richard sitting on the bedside table.

"What's to do? Grandmother said he's returned to Princeton for the semester."

"You should have let him come up to see you."

"I talked to him on the phone and promised to see him when he comes home for the holidays. And naturally, we'll keep writing each other."

"Why are you being so stubborn?"

"Why are you asking so many questions? You don't even know him."

Kimbra glanced away. "Maybe not, but I feel sorry for him."

"Why?"

"Because he cares about you and you won't do anything about it. Do you know what I'd give to have a boyfriend?"

Jenny shook her head. "If only it were true. No . . . Richard's only a friend. I came to grips with that a long time ago."

"But you love him, don't you?"

Jenny colored. "The Jenny I used to be loved him. But I was different then. I was well. Now that I'm sick, loving someone, burdening someone with my life, seems unfair."

Kimbra stepped backward, looking incredulous. "That's one of the dumbest things I've ever heard pass your lips, Jenny Crawford! Are you saying that sick people shouldn't fall in love?"

Jenny felt flustered. "I'm saying Richard has a regular life and doesn't need me messing it up. He always looked out for me when we were growing up, but now it's my turn to look out for him. I know that girls are crazy about Richard. I know he can have any one of them he wants. He shouldn't be stuck with me out of some sense of family loyalty."

"You might give him a say," Kimbra counseled.

"Maybe if I stay in remission, I will." Jenny patted Kimbra's shoulder. "Don't keep your parents waiting. Go have a life."

"I'll call and write," Kimbra promised, and re-treated from the room.

Without her friends, the room seemed empty and hollow, and although she realized that their beds would soon be occupied by new patients, no one could ever take their place in her heart.

When Jenny came home to her grandmother's, leaves were tinged with gold and streaked with red, the air was crisp, the sky a brilliant blue. As the chauffeured limo pulled up and parked in front of the pre–Civil War mansion, Jenny saw the house staff waiting on the brick steps. Each of them greeted her as Barry, the driver, carried her into the house and up the long, winding staircase to her room. The familiar scents of the old house—smells of lemon wax, freshly laundered linen, and cut flowers—told Jenny she was home, and evoked the golden comforts of her childhood.

Her grandmother climbed the stairs first, threw open Jenny's bedroom door, and chided Barry to be careful. A large banner welcoming her home was strung from corner to corner and attached to the crown molding of the ceiling, and vases of flowers adorned the dresser, her desk, and both windowsills.

"It's so good to have you back," Grandmother said after Barry had settled Jenny beneath the lace-trimmed covers of her canopy bed. "Are you hungry? Is there anything you want?"

Overcome by emotion, Jenny only shook her head. Looking around at the things she'd taken for granted all her life, Jenny felt as if she were seeing them for the first time. How lucky she was to have so much! Not only material things, but the love and care of a woman such as her grandmother. "I have everything I want," Jenny replied.

Marian smiled. "I've hired a Mrs. Hunter to tutor you. She has excellent credentials, but if she's not to your liking—"

"She'll be fine." Jenny inhaled the sweet aromas of home and sank back against her pillows. Outside one of her windows, she saw the leafy branches of an old maple tree. "The leaves were green when I left for the hospital," she observed. "Now, fall's coming."

"I know." Her grandmother's voice sounded wistful.

"I guess this is how Rip Van Winkle must have felt when he woke up to see that the world had changed."

"Probably.... But you're home now, and soon you'll be as active as ever. I'm having the tennis courts resurfaced come next spring. I know how you like to play."

Jenny hadn't thought about a game of tennis in months. "I'm afraid Monopoly's more my speed these days."

"You'll be back in form in no time," Grandmother countered with a wave of her hand. She opened Jenny's suitcase and began putting things away.

"Why don't you let Mrs. McCully do that?" Jenny named the housekeeper who'd been with her grandmother since before Jenny had lived with her.

"Not today," Grandmother said. "I don't wish to share the pleasure."

Jenny's heart filled to overflowing. "I'm so glad I'm home," she said. "So glad."

Grandmother set the silver-framed photo of Richard atop a graceful cherrywood table next to Jenny's bed. "I thought you might like this near you. You've carted it around for months."

Jenny gazed longingly at Richard aboard his sail-boat. "Yes."

"According to his father, Richard seems to have turned over a new leaf. He's buckling down at school and actually seems to be taking his studies seriously."

"That's great." The information both surprised and pleased Jenny. She'd always known that he was smart and capable.

"Richard and Dorothy aren't sure why he's done an about-face, but they are pleased." Grandmother smiled indulgently. "I guess sooner or later, everyone has to grow up, even Richard Holloway the Third."

Seventeen

Dear Jenny,
Winter seems to come so much earlier up here in
Vermont. Thanksgiving is barely over, and already
it's freezing cold. But enough about our dumb
weather. Your last letter really meant a lot to me. I
don't know why, but ever since I came home from
the hospital, I've felt so "out of it."
Maybe it's because I'm being bused this year to the
new high school. I swear, ninth grade isn't at all
like middle school. The other girls have their own
little cliques, and I don't feel like I fit in with a single one. I know they think I'm contaminated because I've had cancer. I overheard some of them
talking, and they think they can catch leukemia
from me. How dumb!
I heard from Noreen last week, and she sure sounds
down. I don't think she's doing well at all. Her
handwriting looks so shaky. Oh, about Christmas—I can't come to visit. My grandparents in

California want us to fly out for the holidays. They even sent us plane tickets. We're going to Disneyland. I don't mind seeing Mickey Mouse, but I'll miss being one of the Four Musketeers (or is it the Four Horsemen of Destruction?).

Keep writing. Your letters mean a lot. You, Noreen, and Kimbra are the only ones who understand me. Love and stuff,
Elaine

JENNY FOLDED ELAINE's letter thoughtfully. She too was worried about Noreen. The last time they'd talked on the phone, Noreen had sounded groggy and drugged. "It's my pain medicine," Noreen said. "I hurt all the time, but my doctor says I don't need to go back to the hospital. My mom cries a lot when she doesn't know I'm listening. Sometimes, I get the feeling that everyone's trying to hide something from me."

Jenny called Kimbra, caught her coming in from school, and read her Elaine's letter.

"I understand the prejudice bit," Kimbra said. "I get it all the time. You're lucky you have a tutor and don't have to face the high school rat race every day."

Jenny didn't feel so lucky. Because of her private tutor, she was certainly caught up with her class academically, and in some subjects, she was even ahead. But studying at home left her restless and bored. "I guess either way has its pros and cons," she replied. "You sound angry. What's up?"

"I never could fool you," Kimbra admitted with a sigh. "I talked with the basketball coach yesterday and told her I wanted to go out for the team. I'm still a good shooter from the foul line, and as I told her, I wouldn't have my hands all over the opponents and get called for fouling by the refs."

"And?"

"And she almost fainted. It seems no high school in Maryland has ever had a one-armed ball player. Can you imagine that?"

Jenny chuckled. "If anyone can be the first, it'll be you."

"Over the school board's dead bodies."

"What do you mean?"

"They won't let me play. They says it's 'too risky' for my health."

"But you're perfectly healthy. No more tumors."

"I know, but they aren't listening. My dad's fighting mad, and he says he's going to get an attorney and take the whole school board to court if need be."

Jenny wished she could console Kimbra. "I can tell my grandmother. Maybe her attorney can recommend a good lawyer to take your case."

"That's nice of you, but I'd rather not become a media event. It's bad enough that I'm different from everyone else. I don't really want my troubles aired in the newspapers and on local TV."

"Maybe the board will change its mind."

"I doubt it. I guess I should just give it up."

"Don't do that." Jenny was surprised by the vehemence in her own voice.

"Why not?"

"Because you can't let them push you around. Because if you don't fight now, it'll be harder to fight next time."

There was a pause as Kimbra thought over what Jenny had said. Finally, she broke the quiet. "I'll think about it. I'll talk to my parents."

"Good." Jenny toyed with the phone wire. "Are we still on for Christmas?"

"As far as I know. What do you hear from Noreen?"

Jenny shared her concerns about their friend. "I wanted to go over and see her last weekend, but her mother said no, that she wasn't up to visitors."

"Maybe we can both go visit when I come at Christmastime." Kimbra cleared her throat. "So, what do you hear from the hunk?"

"You mean Richard?" Jenny asked with a laugh. "He's doing great. He wrote to say that he's in danger of making the dean's list this semester."

"That's a danger?"

"If he does, his parents will expect him to make it every time."

"Yeah, I see the problem. Will you see him at Christmas?"

"Yes. I'm over my recluse period. Besides, I almost look human again. My hair's almost an inch long. If I slather it with gel and comb it straight up, I look like a porcupine."

"Very funny." Kimbra giggled into the receiver. "Why don't you buy a wig for yourself?"

"I did, and I hate it. It's hot and makes my scalp itch. No, either I wear the real thing or go bald. I do know one hundred and one ways to tie a scarf, however, so this experience hasn't been a total waste."

"You always have been able to look on the bright side." They shared another laugh, then Kimbra asked, "How're your maintenance treatments?"

"I go in every few weeks, but I never get used to the chemo and how sick it makes me. At least, the stuff is milder than what they dumped in me when I was in the hospital, so now I'm only sick for about a day. No new blasts in my blood work, and that's a relief. I don't think I could endure another stint in the hospital. Especially not without my three cellmates."

"Well, if you're reconfined, I'll visit you, but there's no way they'll lock me up in that place again. No way."

The next time Jenny went in for a treatment, she decided to visit the pediatric oncology floor, something she hadn't done since checking out in September. When she stepped off the elevator, she was struck by how much the same everything looked and sounded—the gaily painted murals, the checkered linoleum, the clatter of dish carts, the hurrying nurses. She had been prepared to feel revulsion for the whole atmosphere, but was surprised to feel a sense of identification and belonging.

She peeked inside the activity room. Christmas decorations, strings of lights, and paper chains brightened the playroom. Except for a few kids playing video games and the TV blaring out cartoons, there wasn't anything going on. A Christmas tree in the corner was lit up, and its branches looked so burdened with handmade decorations that she wondered why it hadn't fallen over.

She recalled her art therapy sessions with her friends and smiled. In spite of it all, she had had a few good times in the hospital. *But it was because of my friends*, she reminded herself. If it hadn't been for them, she would have gone stir-crazy.

Jenny thought about doing something nice for them, something to show her gratitude for their friendship, but at the moment, her mind drew a blank. Maybe when Kimbra came for her visit right after Christmas, Jenny could do something special for her. Too bad that Elaine couldn't come. Not to mention Noreen.

She pushed aside her concerns over Noreen because she didn't want to think about her friend's prognosis. *What did the doctors know?* she asked herself. Noreen could beat their odds, their gloom-and-doom predictions. Hadn't Kimbra? And both she and Elaine were doing fine. Everybody who got cancer didn't automatically die from it. With the start of 1979 just around the corner, they were all going to have a good year. . . .

A spray of cartoon bullets from the TV set jerked Jenny out of her thoughts. She glanced at her watch and realized she was late for her chemo treatment. She dreaded it. She was guaranteed a twenty-four-hour spell of vomiting afterward. "Get moving," she told herself under her breath.

This would be her last treatment until after New Year's. She looked forward to the weeks of feeling human and of forgetting she was still in therapy. At the end of the week, Richard would be home. Her heart skipped a beat when she thought about seeing him. Of course, she still didn't look like her former self, but she didn't look like death warmed over either. The dark cliché made her smile.

Richard. Jenny hurried down to the outpatient therapy wing of the hospital, her thoughts and her heart full of hope for his homecoming.

Eighteen

❧

"THE ANGEL'S LOPSIDED, Timothy. Straighten her up."

Jenny sat on the floor of her grandmother's enormous living room, sorting through boxes of ornaments and listening to Marian issue instructions to the house staff. Above her, balancing on a ladder, Timothy, one of the handymen, struggled to please her grandmother's discerning eye.

"Yes . . . that's better," she heard Marian say. "Now, make sure one of the lights is positioned directly behind her. I want it to appear as if she's glowing."

Jenny smiled to herself. It was like this every year. Grandmother cracking the whip, the staff scurrying to do her bidding. Jenny looked up at the magnificent evergreen that filled the corner of the room and brushed the top of the ceiling with its branches. This was her grandmother's tree, the formal one, decorated more splendidly than any Jenny had ever seen.

Yet, Jenny's personal favorite was the tree down in

the rumpus room, the one for just her and her grandmother and their gifts for one another. This was the tree that contained her handmade ornaments and those of her father, left over from when he'd been a boy. This was the tree that she took personal responsibility for decorating every year. She lifted the flap of a box and pulled out a crumpled wreath. "What's this?" she asked, holding it up.

"I believe it's the wreath you made while you were in the hospital last summer," Grandmother said, coming beside her.

"You *saved* this dumb thing?"

"Don't look so shocked." Grandmother rescued it from Jenny's grasp. "I think it's quite charming."

"It looks awful."

"No, it doesn't. I'm hanging it over the mantel, where the evergreen branches meet in the center." Grandmother gestured toward the huge brick fireplace, where Mrs. McCully was busy draping pine branches and holly sprigs across the old oak mantel. Grandmother walked the wreath over and handed it to the housekeeper. "I think it will look charming as the focal point."

"No, it won't," Jenny protested. "It's junky."

Grandmother gave her an arching look. "This is my room to decorate, remember? You have your own."

Jenny offered an exasperated sigh, but deep down, it touched her that her handmade wreath would have a place of honor over the mantel. By that evening, the house would be filled with people attending her grandmother's annual Christmas party, and they would all see the wreath. "I'm going to decorate *my* tree," Jenny announced, scooping up a string of bubble lights. "And if any of your guests asks where you found that old thing, please say I made it when I was ten instead of sixteen!"

That night, Jenny put on a dress of midnight blue velvet. She tied a blue silk scarf streaked with threads of gold and silver around her head and pulled wispy bangs over her forehead. "You look lovely," Grandmother said.

"Thanks," Jenny replied, caring only what Richard would think of her.

The doorbell rang all evening as guests arrived. Jenny smiled politely during numerous introductions, but never stopped watching the doorway for the Holloways. When she saw Dorothy sweep into the foyer, her heart wedged in her throat.

Richard stood behind his parents on the living room threshold, looking reserved. Jenny felt her knees go weak. He was even more handsome than she remembered. She longed to run forward and throw her arms around him, but she knew she couldn't.

His gaze traveled the room, then locked on to hers. The party, the music, the noise all faded as their eyes held. Slowly, he stepped around his parents and came toward her, and she walked forward to meet him in the center of the crowded room.

"You're beautiful," he said, looking down at her. "How have you been?"

"I'm fine. And you? How's your term going?" She wanted to throw herself in his arms. She wanted to hold him and never let go.

"I don't take my exams until January, but I think I'm doing all right."

The polite exchange had her nerves on edge. Even their letters were more personal than this. "My studies are going well too. I'm hoping to be back in regular classes when the new term begins."

He glanced over his shoulder. "There are a lot of people here. Can we go some place more private?"

"There's the rumpus room. I haven't quite finished decorating down there yet, but it's quiet."

She led the way down the stairs into a cozy room lined with pine paneling and carpeted in bright red. Timothy had laid a fire in the fireplace, and its flames danced brightly. She crossed to the tree and fingered the needles. "The other tree's fancier, but this one's my favorite."

He reached out and touched one of the decorations. "This tree's better in a lot of ways," he said.

Jenny's heart was hammering hard, and because the room was so quiet, she was fearful he might hear it. "What will you be doing during the holidays?" She wanted him to ask if they could spend time together, do things with each other, no matter how trivial.

"My father's dragging me down to the Bahamas on a weeklong fishing trip the day after Christmas."

"You're leaving?" She averted her eyes, hoping to hide her disappointment. He'd gone off and left her last Christmas.

"The trip has a purpose," he said with a sigh. "These fishing buddies of Dad's are prominent attorneys, and he thinks that my meeting them will give me an edge in getting into law school when I apply. Getting into one of the top Ivy League schools isn't easy."

"Law school? Last summer, you said you hated the idea of being a lawyer. When did you change your mind?"

"Later in the summer." He lifted her chin with his

forefinger, and his gaze burned into hers. "After I worked at the firm, I saw that some aspects of law interested me. I can become a good lawyer if I put my mind to it."

Staring into the green depths of his eyes, having him so close, smelling of bayberry and fresh pine, was almost making her crazy. "You never told me that in your letters."

"There was a lot I couldn't say in my letters."

"Are you angry with me because I wouldn't let you come see me when I was in the hospital going through chemo? That I insisted on using the mail?"

"Yes." He said the word flatly, causing her stomach to constrict. "You hurt me."

"I never meant to hurt you. I was so sick. I was out of it for so much of the time. In ICU, I remember being afraid I would never see you again, and the feeling was horrible. By the time I got well enough to return to my room, you'd gone back to school."

"We've been friends for years, Jenny. You shouldn't have kept me away."

"Will you forgive me? Can we still be friends?" She saw the muscles working in his jaw. He lowered his hand, but her skin couldn't forget where his touch had lain.

"I'll always be your friend. But friends don't leave friends out. Friends share ... good and bad."

His lecture stung. She must seem more like a child to him than ever before. All at once, the age difference between them loomed like a gulf. "Well, if I relapse, I'll let you come up for a visit."

"Don't even tease about that happening." His eyes were serious, his tone hard.

She realized he'd never find her dark humor

amusing the way Kimbra, Noreen, and Elaine had. *Why should he?* she thought. Richard was healthy and had never known the inside of her world. "I didn't mean it literally. I was only trying to tell you I'm sorry I acted so weird while I was hospitalized."

Richard reached out and stroked her cheek with the back of his hand. "Please, don't shut me out again."

Her heart fairly leapt out of her chest. "It's a promise." She allowed herself to look up into his face, and for an instant, she saw something there she couldn't read. Was it longing? Concern? Pity? She didn't want his pity. She took a step backward. "So you'll be out in the Atlantic Ocean on New Year's Eve. Sounds like a nice place to welcome 1979."

"It would be better if I were on the *Triple H* with a beautiful girl instead of with a bunch of old guys smelling like fish." He walked to the fireplace, and with his hands shoved deep in his pockets, he stared into the flames. "What will you do?" he asked. "Didn't you write that one of your hospital roommates was coming for a visit?"

"Kimbra was supposed to come, but now she can't."

"What happened?"

"Let's sit down," Jenny said, "and I'll tell you."

Nineteen

Richard sat on the sofa with Jenny, making certain that he kept to one far end. He was afraid of getting any closer. If he did, he might not be able to control his impulses. All he wanted to do, all he'd wanted the whole evening, was to pull her into his arms. She looked fragile to him, her skin pale as ivory. And she was thin, as delicate as fine crystal. "Tell me about your friend," he said.

"It's good news really." Jenny tucked her feet under herself on the sofa. "The school board was giving Kimbra a hard time about playing basketball. They didn't want a one-armed girl on the team, but that's discrimination, you know."

Jenny looked so offended on Kimbra's behalf that Richard grinned. "I know. I worked in a law firm."

She smiled sheepishly. "Anyway, her parents had a fit and threatened a lawsuit, so the board put a bunch of restrictions on Kimbra. They wouldn't tell her no, but they wanted to make it so difficult that she'd give up."

"But she didn't?"

"Not Kimbra. She passed all their tests. In fact, she's the best shooter in the entire school, one-armed or otherwise. A couple of weeks ago, she was contacted by some coach who heads up a sports camp for handicapped kids. He'd read about Kimbra in the papers." Jenny spread the hem of her dress so that the blue velvet fell like a curtain over the edge of the cushion.

"This coach invited her to his camp, said it wasn't for wimps, said he'd be tough on her . . . but that if she did well, he'd go to her school board and fight for her to be allowed on the team." Jenny clapped gleefully. "Isn't that great? I wish you could meet Kimbra. You'd really like her."

Richard recalled Kimbra vividly from the night he met her in ICU, but of course, he couldn't tell Jenny, or she'd know how he'd hovered at her bedside when she'd been unconscious. "I hope things work out for her." He picked a loose thread from a pillow.

"Maybe she can visit over spring break. Will you come home, or run off to Florida like so much of the college crowd does?"

"It depends."

"On what?"

On if you're well, he almost blurted. "On what's happening here at home," he said carefully. "I may put in a week at Dad's firm."

"You're really serious about practicing law, aren't you?"

"Very serious."

"You must have had some revelation this summer," Jenny said with a laugh. "I remember when all you wanted to do was sail around the world."

"People change."

She dropped her gaze self-consciously, concentrating on her hands folded in her lap. "You can say that again."

Once again, he lifted her chin. "Have you changed?"

"I . . . look . . . different . . . now." She found the words difficult to say.

Suddenly, he couldn't control his urge to touch her any longer. Gently, he tugged at the scarf. She recoiled. "Trust me," he begged. "Please."

Her heart thudded, but she didn't pull away a second time. *Trust him!* She felt him slide the scarf from her head, felt it flutter over her shoulders. Without the scarf's covering, her head felt cool and exposed. She resisted the urge to cover her crop of dark fuzz with her hands. "It's growing back," she said nervously. "It'll just take some time."

His fingers brushed through the downy fuzz. "It's soft," he said. "Really soft."

She felt unexpected tears brim in her eyes, as an overwhelming sense of loss swept through her—not for her hair, but for her summer, her health, her innocence. "It was horrible, Richard." Her voice came out in a whispered crack. "All the needles, all the pain . . . it was so horrible." As if a dam had opened, Jenny wept. She clung to him, and he stroked her once long, dark, beautiful hair. She expected to feel naked and vulnerable, but in his arms, she experienced protection and shelter.

"Jenny . . . Jenny . . ." he whispered. His arms wrapped around her, and she sank against his chest.

His heart thumped beneath her cheek. "I wish I could have been with you."

Richard wished he could soak up her pain, blot out the terrible memories. He felt frustrated and impotent. All he could do was hold her and let her cry it out. He wanted to tell her that he loved her, that he would be there for her no matter what, but he didn't know how.

"Jenny. Are you down there, dear?" Marian Crawford's voice called from the top of the rumpus room stairs.

Quickly, Jenny pulled away from Richard, wiping her tear-stained cheeks hurriedly. "I'm here, Grandmother," Jenny called.

Richard willed Marian to go away, but she came downstairs, halting at the bottom, surveying the room with one piercing glance. "You're crying." Marian shot Richard a threatening look.

"I don't know what's wrong with me," Jenny said, fumbling with a tissue box on an end table. "We came down here to talk, to catch up on things, and I fell to pieces."

Richard was beside Jenny in an instant. "It's my fault. I started her talking about the hospital."

Another scathing look from Marian. "Why don't you freshen up, dear," she told Jenny. "Go up the back way through the kitchen. I'll be up in a minute."

"I don't want to ruin your party," Jenny said.

"Nonsense. It's my party, and you can cry if you want to." Jenny smiled shakily over her grandmother's humor. "Now, run along."

Jenny cast Richard a longing glance, and he nodded, urging her to go on. "We'll talk later," he promised. She hurried up the stairs, and he followed, passing Marian as he went.

Marian's hand darted out and caught Richard's arm. "You be careful, Richard. Don't hurt her," Marian warned. "I won't stand for it." Her eyes looked steely blue as she spoke.

Richard pulled away from her grasp and held her gaze. "I'm not your enemy, Mrs. Crawford. We're on the same side. We both want what's best for Jenny." He stepped around Marian and took the stairs two at a time.

At the top, he reentered the lively party crowd. In the corner, the magnificent Christmas tree rose loftily and glittered like a jewel. *This is Jenny's world,* he told himself ruefully. Sick or well, this was the world she had been born to. He felt he would forever be an outsider.

The only thing that broke up Jenny's monotonous days was sitting for a formal portrait painted in oil by one of New England's most noted artists. It was part of her Christmas gift from her grandmother.

At first, Jenny had thought the idea silly, but once she met the artist, and caught his enthusiasm for his work, she warmed to the project. He posed her in her blue velvet gown in the library beside the magnificent arched window that spilled winter sunlight into the room. She posed for two hours daily, at the same time each day, so that the light would remain constant.

"Where will you hang it?" she asked her grandmother, who often attended the sittings.

"Why, over the mantel, of course."

"But Grandfather's portrait's there."

"It's time to hang him in the hall with the rest of

the Crawfords. It's time for youth and beauty to watch over this old relic."

"He may not like being rehung," Jenny teased.

Grandmother waved her hand. "Posh. I'll hang him where I choose. He can argue with me in eternity if he doesn't approve."

Jenny also asked about returning to school full-time.

"I'd rather you not," Grandmother said. "The tutor is eager to work with you once more, and besides, you're doing so well with her guidance. I see no need for you to return to the classroom."

Jenny felt as if she should put up an argument, but she honestly didn't have the heart for one. She remembered Elaine's difficult adjustment in returning to school. She recalled the stories Kimbra had told her over the phone. "People talk behind my back," Kimbra had said. "They whisper about me and treat me like I'm a freak. I wish there were someway I could hide my problem. It's the pits not being normal, not being able to fit in."

Kids could be thoughtless and cruel, and Jenny didn't want to be treated that way at her school. If she worked hard and stayed on grade level, then she could return next fall. Surely, she'd be completely recovered by then. Her leukemia would be a thing of the past and, therefore, of no interest to the girls who liked to gossip. She told her grandmother, "I don't mind being tutored this term, but when I'm a senior, I want to attend regular classes."

"Absolutely," Grandmother agreed. "When you're a senior, after this whole experience is behind you, you can do anything you want."

By February, the artist was putting the finishing touches on Jenny's portrait, and she was growing excited because Richard had written that he'd be spending spring break at home.

"You have a phone call, Jennifer," Mrs. McCully called up the stairs one afternoon, following her sitting.

Hoping it might be Kimbra or Elaine, Jenny eagerly picked up the receiver. "Jenny here," she announced.

"This is Shannon—Noreen's sister. Do you remember me?"

"Of course." Jenny felt her stomach constrict because Shannon had no reason to call her. "What's wrong? Is Noreen back in the hospital?"

Shannon started crying. "Noreen passed away last night. She made me promise that I'd call her friends when it happened. Her funeral's the day after tomorrow."

Twenty

~

JENNY PEERED OUT of the darkened limousine, at the lighted front of the funeral home. People streamed in and out of the large double doors, friends of Noreen's family, paying their last respects. Now that she was actually here, Jenny hesitated to go inside. How could she endure seeing her friend lying in a coffin?

"I hate being here." Elaine sat in the seat across from her, sniffing.

"It's bad, all right," Kimbra said beside her, "but at least, we're here together."

Jenny's insistence on attending had caused one of the worst arguments she'd ever had with her grandmother. "There's no reason for you to go," Marian had said. "We'll send flowers—as large a basket as you want."

"Not go! You're not serious! I have to go. She was my friend."

"I won't hear of it."

"Then I'll catch the subway and go. You can't keep me away."

"Funerals are depressing."

"Tell me about it! I was there when we buried my parents, remember?" The words had hurt her grandmother. Jenny saw her wince, but didn't back down. "I'm going."

"Then I'll go with you."

"I don't want you to go with me!" Jenny had shouted. "I don't need you smothering me. This is something I want to do alone, so please don't come along! You're not doing me any favors."

In the end, Jenny had her way, and in an effort to smooth over their fight, Grandmother had arranged to fly in both Elaine and Kimbra, and to have them spend a few days with Jenny following the funeral. They'd come straight to the funeral home from the airport. "I've never met anyone who had her own chauffeur before," Kimbra said when the limo had pulled up to the curb and Barry loaded their luggage.

"The car belongs to my grandmother," Jenny replied, feeling as if she should apologize. When they'd all been in the hospital together, they had been equals, but now, her wealth set her apart and made her self-conscious.

Elaine pulled some makeup from her purse and dabbed it on, while Jenny stared out at the looming entrance of the building.

"Forget it," Kimbra growled. "Noreen can't appreciate it, and no one else cares."

Elaine began to sob, and Jenny put her arm around her. "Don't be mean, Kimbra. This is hard enough on all of us without snide remarks."

"Sorry," Kimbra replied contritely, slinking down into the seat.

Barry opened the car door, and Jenny scrambled out. Patches of snow and ice on the ground shone in the artificial lights of the parking lot. "Wait for us, please," Jenny told him.

The three of them made their way slowly up the walkway of the funeral parlor, holding each other's hands. They stepped into the foyer. Soft music played, and weeping could be heard coming from various rooms.

"This way," Jenny said, reading Noreen's name and room number on a wall directory.

"This is all so bizarre," Kimbra grumbled. "Like taking a ticket to see a show."

"Shush," Elaine demanded. "Show some respect."

Jenny's heart was thudding, and she felt queasy. Her grandmother had been right—she shouldn't have come. She stepped into a room packed with people. Chairs lined the walls, and she recognized Noreen's parents sitting and crying softly as people came over and whispered condolences to them.

"I feel sick," Elaine muttered.

"Don't you dare," Kimbra warned. "We're all in this together."

Jenny swallowed her own taste of sickness and strained to see through the groups of people. In the very front of the room, she spied baskets and wreaths of flowers and the edge of a coffin. "I can't go up there. I can't go look at her body."

The three of them clung together, afraid to move. Shannon emerged from a small cluster of mourners. "You're here," she said, greeting them like long lost friends. "Please, come see Mom and Dad. They've been asking about you."

"They have?" Jenny was surprised.

Shannon led them over to her parents. Noreen's

mother reached up and grasped Jenny's hand. "It's so good of the three of you to come. Your friendships meant so much to my darling girl. Your calls, your letters—well, they brought her such pleasure in the midst of all her pain."

Kimbra and Elaine mumbled their thanks, but Jenny felt weighed down by guilt. Sure, she'd called and written, but she had also lived right across town and had never come over for a visit. Elaine and Kimbra had an excuse—they lived in other states— but Jenny felt ashamed.

Why hadn't she come? She planned to, but had never followed through. *Because I didn't believe Noreen would really die.* The answer came to her with sobering clarity. "I—I'm sorry I didn't see her before ... before ..." Jenny heard herself say.

"It's just as well," Noreen's mother said, dabbing her eyes with a handkerchief. "She was so very ill at the end, and in such terrible pain."

"No more pain now, Ma," Shannon said.

Jenny felt numb and woodenly backed away. She felt Kimbra take her by the elbow and heard her whisper, "Let's get this over with."

Huddled together, the three friends walked toward the coffin. Jenny's heart hammered, and her feet felt leaden. Baskets and bouquets lined the floor surrounding a coffin covered by a mantle of pink roses. Inside a polished blue casket, Noreen rested on a bed of white satin. Jenny heard Elaine gasp and begin crying harder.

Her own eyes were dry, as if she'd passed beyond feeling, beyond emotions. She'd become a camera, simply recording pictures and scenes. She wasn't a part of this event. She was removed, floating above it.

Noreen was dressed in white, and in her folded

hands, she held a crucifix. "Her confirmation dress," Jenny heard someone say in passing. "Doesn't she look like a sleeping angel?"

"White should be reserved for brides," Kimbra remarked stonily.

"She would have preferred red," Elaine added, between sobs.

"Let's get out of here," Jenny said, pulling them toward the door. She knew she couldn't stand to be trapped in that room another moment. Noreen wasn't there—only a waxlike substitute of her.

Jenny hurried outside into the biting cold air. Her teeth chattered, but she was drenched in sweat. "Are you all right, Miss?" Barry asked.

"Just get us home, please" she replied, desperately trying to hold back tears. Once they were on the road, she allowed herself to weep. "It's not fair," she murmured.

"None of it's fair," Kimbra said, "but it's the way things are."

When Barry pulled the car into the long driveway, both Elaine and Kimbra stared out of the window openmouthed. The great mansion was lit with floodlights, and the massive front doors gleamed with brass accents. "You live here?" Kimbra asked.

Again, Jenny's defenses surfaced. "It's my grandmother's—been in the family for generations."

Grandmother greeted them cordially, but Jenny thought Marian clung to her a fraction too long. She didn't want to be treated like a baby in front of her friends, so she pulled away quickly. "I've had Timothy set up extra beds in your room," Grandmother announced. "And Mrs. McCully has laid out snacks on your bureau, so please, relax and enjoy yourselves."

All the way up the winding staircase, Kimbra and Elaine kept their gazes darting every which way, and when they were alone in Jenny's spacious bedroom, Elaine blurted, "Cripes, I had no idea you were a freaking Rockefeller! Have you been rich all your life?"

"Only after I was seven . . . after my folks were killed." Jenny hoped to stem a flood of questions by reminding them that she was an orphan and hadn't been born to this luxury.

Kimbra tossed her purse on one of the rollaway beds. "Noreen would have loved it. To think you lived with us in the ward all that time, and her little nose for news never got wind of it."

"I didn't see that it made any difference between us. We were all sick. It—it doesn't matter to either of you, does it?"

Kimbra and Elaine looked at one another. "Not to me," Elaine said. "You're right—we were all sick."

"Yeah . . . cancer, the great equalizer," Kimbra mumbled.

Elaine helped herself to a cola and chocolate chip cookies from the sumptuous tray Mrs. McCully had prepared. "That viewing business at the funeral home was the pits. When I die, promise you all won't come stand over my coffin and stare at me."

"Promise me you won't die until we're all too old to travel," Kimbra countered.

Jenny sat heavily on her lace-trimmed coverlet. "I wish Noreen were here. This sleepover is something she should be a part of."

"She would have loved it," Kimbra said, poking her head into Jenny's private bathroom. "No lines for the toilet."

Tears started trickling down Elaine's cheeks. "I

miss her. She was the first friend I made in the hospital."

"She wouldn't want us to sit around bawling," Kimbra said, handing Elaine a tissue.

"You're right," Jenny concurred. "It's time to send in the clowns."

"What's that mean?" Elaine blew her nose.

"It's an old circus trick. Whenever some disaster happens under the big top, the ringmaster sends in clowns to divert the audience's attention." Jenny raised a glass of cola. "Here's to Noreen. I hope she's happy in heaven."

"To Noreen." Kimbra and Elaine joined in the toast.

Jenny set her glass down. "You know what makes me feel bad? I never gave Noreen that party."

"What party?"

"The one I promised her the night before her surgery."

"I remember." Elaine munched on a cookie. "In spite of it all, we had some good times, didn't we?"

Jenny gazed thoughtfully at both her friends. "You know, I could still throw her a party."

"How?"

Thoughts tumbled wildly in Jenny's mind. "It's something I could do *for* her, something I could do for all the kids trapped in that hospital." A plan took shape in her mind. "And you can help me. It'll be our tribute to Noreen. It'll be such a bash that no one will ever forget her."

"Couldn't that cost a bundle?" Elaine asked.

"So what? Remember—I'm as rich as a 'freaking Rockefeller.'"

Twenty-One

"WHAT KIND OF bash should it be?" Elaine scrambled up on Jenny's bed eagerly. "Think about how many little kids are stuck in the hospital. It should be something that is right for them too."

A radio commercial about Ringling Brothers–Barnum and Bailey Circus coming to Boston Gardens in late spring played on the radio. "We'll have a private mini circus," Jenny announced. "A big top. Animals. Clowns. Carnival rides—the whole works."

"Like how? Have a private performance down at the Gardens and bus the kids in?"

"Some are too sick to leave the hospital," Kimbra said. "That wouldn't be fair."

Jenny thought for a moment. "I know—we'll set up the circus on the hospital grounds, in the parking lots, right there on the premises. That way, jugglers and clowns and special acts can go up to the floors for those kids who positively can't leave the building. The others can have their own private performance. Their families can come, and Noreen's family can be the guests of honor." Jenny's mind was racing so fast that the ideas tumbled out on top of one another.

"How can we pull this off?" Kimbra wanted to know.

"With my grandmother's help, we can do it."

"Your grandmother?"

Jenny flashed an impish smile. "I don't know anybody who can say no to Grandmother."

Marian Crawford listened intently to their plans the next morning, studying Jenny's face as she laid out their scheme. "I haven't seen you this enthusiastic about anything in months," Marian said over a cup of hot tea.

"I haven't felt this enthusiastic about anything in months," Jenny admitted.

"You really want to do this?"

"More than anything I've wanted in a long time."

"It won't be easy, but I'm not without contacts in this city."

Jenny grinned. "I figured you'd know the right people." She leaned over the table, glancing around at Kimbra and Elaine, who were over at the sideboard scooping up helpings of scrambled eggs and brown bread from silver chafing dishes. "You told me I had a trust fund that will one day be mine. Can I spent some of that money now on this?"

She saw a film of moisture cloud her grandmother's eyes. Marian cleared her throat and set down her china teacup in its fragile saucer. "Dear Jenny, that won't be necessary."

"But you shouldn't have to spend your money on my harebrained ideas."

"One of the reasons the rich stay rich is because

they know how to get other rich people to *donate* what they want." Marian patted Jenny's hand and smiled indulgently. "We won't spend any more money of ours than is absolutely necessary, Jenny. It's an unwritten code."

Jenny laughed long and hard.

"What's so funny?" Kimbra asked.

"Learning how to be rich," Jenny replied. "It seems I've got a lot to learn." She reached out and took her grandmother's hand. "But I have the perfect teacher."

Each day, Jenny hurried through her lessons with her tutor, then rushed to her grandmother's study, where a special secretary Marian had hired worked on the project. They arranged for the circus to arrive in Boston two days early for a special hospital presentation, and local newspaper and television reporters publicized the story.

Jenny designed special posters, saw that they were printed, and personally carried them up to the hospital and posted them on every floor. She talked to Kimbra and Elaine almost every night. One evening when the phone rang, she grabbed the receiver and heard Richard's voice.

"What's going on up there? I turned on the national news in the frat house and heard about some circus coming to Boston Children's Hospital. And your grandmother's name kept being mentioned."

Just the sound of his voice made Jenny feel warm all over. "You mean you got your head out of the books long enough to see what was going on in the real world?"

He laughed. "I apologize for turning into a scholar. Believe me, being a playboy's a whole lot more fun."

She told him about how the event was intended as a memorial to Noreen. "But so many people have sent in donations after seeing the kids from the hospital on TV that we've raised a bundle of money for cancer research. Even though the cost of the circus is covered, people really want to help in some way."

"Sounds like you've started something big."

His approval meant a lot to her. "It's been fun, and I know it's going to do some good too."

"Is the party private?"

"The kids, their families, and a bunch of reporters are the only ones allowed."

"How about me?"

Her heart skipped a beat. "I can probably get you a ticket. I know the organizers."

He laughed, and the sound sent a melting sensation through her. "Then I'll be there, but only as long as you take me under your wing personally. I won't settle for less."

In late April, the circus roustabouts erected a scaled-down version of the big top on the grounds of Children's Hospital. The weather cooperated, dawning sunny and balmy on the Saturday of the event. "God must approve," Elaine remarked as the three girls watched the men working.

"I'm sure your grandmother had a discussion with him about it," Kimbra observed, making the others laugh.

When Richard strolled over to the group, Jenny forgot her promise to herself about acting her age, and threw her arms around him like an exuberant child. He hugged her in return, and Elaine mimicked a fainting spell behind his back, so that only Jenny and Kimbra could see her antics.

"You remember my friends, don't you?"

Richard greeted them with one of his heart-melting grins. "How did your basketball season turn out?" he asked Kimbra.

"I rode the bench for the first part of the season, but I got my chance when one of our starters got hurt."

"Did you impress your critics?"

Kimbra chuckled. "On the night of my first start, one of my opponents came over and said, 'Just because you're a cripple, don't think I'll go easy on you.'"

"How rude," Elaine said, wrinkling her nose in disgust.

"Psyching out your opponent is part of the game. I didn't mind—it made me feel like I'd be treated as an equal."

"Were you?" Richard asked.

"She knocked me on my butt." Jenny gasped, but Kimbra shook her head. "Rule number one: Don't get mad, get even."

"What did you do?"

"Next time we were up close and personal, I rammed her face with my stump." Kimbra raised her partial arm and grinned innocently. "I broke her nose too."

"Oh, such violence!" Elaine cried, placing her hands over her mouth in mock horror.

"Yeah—aren't I a bad girl?"

The four of them laughed, then Kimbra said, "I never got hassled again, and best of all, my coach was so impressed with the rest of my season that she's sending me to basketball camp this summer.

Not a handicapped kids' camp either, but a regular one."

"Good for you," Richard said, then turned back to Jenny. "How about a tour?"

"Oh, sure," Elaine called as Jenny and Richard walked away. "Leave us alone to face the clowns by ourselves. What kind of friends are you anyway?"

"The best kind," Jenny called back. "Not in your way."

By noon, the grounds swarmed with kids from the hospital and their families—kids in wheelchairs and on crutches, kids bald from chemo and missing limbs. Yet, they were laughing, yelling, having fun. Jenny walked the premises with Richard, feeling a sense of kinship toward them.

Together, she and Richard toured the wards where kids recovering from surgeries or confined to isolation watched circus veterans in wide-eyed wonder. The performers worked fully costumed in sequins and feathers, in elaborate headdresses, in exaggerated makeup, in glitter and greasepaint. She watched the eyes of children reflect disbelief as magicians made objects disappear and reappear; turned water into confetti, bedpans into flowers, IV lines into strings of colorful scarves; and offered up cuddly bunnies from beneath bedcovers. She clapped for clowns who materialized by the dozens from cramped janitorial closets. She helped nurses pass out balloons and popcorn, candy and souvenirs.

That evening, under the tent, she sat with her friends and grandmother and applauded lion tamers, circus ponies, high-wire acts, and a dazzling trio of high-flying trapeze artists. When the performances were over, she went with Richard to the carnival and rode the merry-go-round while he held her hand.

Laughing, they dismounted from painted ponies, and Richard pointed at the glittering Ferris wheel. "Feel up to it?" he asked.

"See you around," she shot back, dashing toward the enormous wheel. They climbed aboard, and she watched the earth fall away as the wheel rose skyward. The weather had turned chilly, but a blanket lay on each seat. Richard pulled it around both their shoulders so that they snuggled warmly beneath it. When the wheel was at the very top, it groaned to a halt.

"What's wrong?" Jenny asked, peering over the side. Below, people looked like ants, and lights glittered like colorful fireflies.

"Not a thing," Richard said.

"But we're stopped."

"I know. I slipped the mechanic ten bucks to give us twenty minutes alone up here."

Twenty-Two

"Ten bucks? Is that all I'm worth?" She joked, but felt flattered. *Alone with Richard on top of the world!* Jenny couldn't think of a single place she'd rather be.

He grinned, but then grew serious. "This circus was really a wonderful idea, Jenny. I've never seen kids look so happy."

"When you've got cancer, you don't usually have much to be happy about. Besides, Grandmother made it all happen."

"Dame Marian did look pretty pleased about the whole thing. I'd say the two of you make a great team."

"I guess . . . my wild ideas and her money."

The sound of calliope music drifted up from the merry-go-round. Richard smoothed her hair, now grown past her jawline. "How are you doing? You know, with your treatments and all."

She felt a black cloud descend. "I go for more

blood work next week. It's like playing Russian roulette. Once my sample of blood is analyzed, will they discover blasts or not? Sometimes, it's all I think about for days before and after the test. And when the 'all-clear' signal comes, I almost faint with gratitude."

"Blasts are the immature cells that signal the return of leukemia, aren't they?"

"Yes," she said, surprised that he knew the term.

"I read everything I could get my hands on when you first got the diagnosis," Richard confessed.

"Then you know that every time a person relapses, it's harder to get back into remission."

"Yes, I know." He recalled his conversations with Marian and the sense of hopelessness he experienced when he realized Jenny's options if chemo and radiation no longer worked.

"It scares me when I think about it. It's hard to think about running out of options," Jenny said.

"So don't think about it." He nestled her against his body. "The hardest thing I ever did was not see you last summer."

"I made a mistake. I see that now, but at the time, I couldn't deal with it."

"It won't happen again?" His question sounded more like a command.

"It won't have to happen again. I'm not going to allow leukemia to return to my body."

He squeezed her shoulders. "That sounds more like it. Don't give up your positive thinking."

She looked to the ground below. "The world looks so different from up here, doesn't it?"

He followed her line of vision. Far in the distance, he saw the lights of Boston Harbor, and beyond that, the dark expanse that he knew was the sea. "Very different."

"I wonder how we look to God. I wonder if he sees us from a different perspective, the way I can see the kids down there. I know so much about them. I know how they feel and what they want. It's an odd sensation." She shook her head to clear out her thoughts and glanced up at Richard's face. Everything inside her yearned to press her lips to his, but she lacked the nerve.

Richard gazed down at Jenny. It took every ounce of his self-control not to kiss her. He knew if he did, their relationship would be forever changed. She'd know his passion, and then there'd be no returning to the safety of their childhood friendship. He feared she might not want to handle the added pressure. Nor would it be fair to require her to deal with their intensified relationship and cancer too. He took a long, shaky breath. "We'll have this summer to make up for last one. It'll be like old times, all right?"

"Sure. Just like old times." She didn't want old times. She wanted him to see her as a woman, not as a girl who was sick. She wanted *him* with all her heart. The Ferris wheel lurched and began to coast downward toward the ground, toward her everyday life.

"Looks like our time's up," he said, "Twenty minutes wasn't long enough. I'll have to remember that if I ever get you alone again."

Alone. The word echoed in her head as the wheel stopped at the bottom and Richard flashed a knowing grin. Her friends would be leaving soon, and so would Richard. Jenny would once again be alone.

* * *

Boston's Logan Airport teemed with people returning from Easter vacation. "You two write to me," Elaine said. "I'm going to miss you both so much." She glanced over her shoulder to the doorway where people were boarding the flight to Burlington, Vermont.

"We will," Kimbra told her.

"Maybe we can get together one time before we go back to school," Jenny suggested.

"I can't." Elaine said. "My parents are sending me to a cancer camp. I'd rather do something with you all, but Mom's making me go."

"You'll have fun," Jenny said halfheartedly. She glanced up and waved. "There's Richard. I guess he finally got the car parked."

"My car keys set off the security alarm, and the security guards had to frisk me," he explained as he reached them. "I'm glad I got here in time to see you off, Elaine."

"You take good care of our friend here," Elaine said, sniffing back tears.

His arm circled Jenny's waist. "No problem."

After another round of hugs, Elaine hurried to join the line of passengers. Jenny turned to Kimbra. "You're next."

"My gate's down that way." Kimbra pointed.

The three of them arrived at the gate for the plane to Baltimore just as the first boarding call was announced. "I'm glad you came," Jenny told her friend.

"I had a great time. Your grandmother's something else—there's nothing she wouldn't do for you, you know."

"I know." Now Jenny felt like bursting into tears. She hated saying good-bye. At least Richard would be around for one more day. She couldn't bear having everyone abandon her at once. "You have fun at that basketball camp."

Kimbra leaned closer. "You have fun in Martha's Vineyard this summer." She lowered her voice to a whisper, and continued, "And let's try and get some action going with the hunk. You know how I count on my friends to help me live romantically through them."

"There's someone out there just for you, Kimbra. I know there is."

"Well, I hope this is the year he finds me." The final boarding call was announced. "Thanks for spreading some of your money around, Jen. I really had a ball."

"There's more where that came from. Maybe we can do something wild and crazy during the holidays, since we didn't get to do anything last year."

"Such as?"

"It's so cold here. Maybe we could all go to Florida."

"Florida!" Kimbra grinned broadly. "Lead me on. We'll look like anemic cucumbers."

The two of them laughed. "What's so funny?" Richard asked.

"Salad," Jenny answered. He looked perplexed, and she and Kimbra giggled. Yet once Kimbra was on the plane and she and Richard were driving home through the snarl of traffic in the Logan Airport tunnel, Jenny felt a lump rise in her throat.

"You okay?" Richard asked, glancing sideways.

"I miss them already."

"Sounds as if you'll all be pretty busy over the summer. Think about going out to the Cape. Things will be different for you this summer."

She knew what he said was true. This summer she could catch up on all the things she missed out on the year before. "You know, the one good thing that came out of this misery has been meeting them. They're the best friends I've ever had." She sighed and leaned against the headrest in Richard's father's Mercedes-Benz. "Noreen too. I miss her every day."

He reached over and took her hand. "Once I come home from college in June, the first thing we'll do is go sailing. We'll pack a picnic lunch, go to the cave and then out on the water. Would you like that?"

"Of course."

"Then think about that. Don't be depressed over what you can't change."

What he said made sense. Nothing could bring Noreen back, and she still had Elaine, Kimbra, and Richard. She squeezed his hand in return. "Write me. I like getting your letters."

"I'll write. You can count on it." He drove back to her grandmother's holding her hand.

Jenny shifted nervously in the chair in Dr. Gallagher's office. "What's taking him so long? How long does it take for him to go over my dumb lab reports?"

"Calm down, dear," her grandmother said soothingly. "Maybe he was paged. He's got a hospital full of patients, and you're an outpatient, so sick people get attended to first."

Jenny chewed her lip. With only two weeks left before they went out to the summer house, she was especially tense. *Don't let anything spoil this summer,* she pleaded silently.

Dr. Gallagher swept into the office. He banged his

chair into his desk and slapped a manila folder against the cluttered top.

"What's wrong?" Jenny felt her heart thudding ominously as she looked at his face.

"Your blood work shows blasts, Jenny. I'm sorry, but you'll have to check back into the hospital."

Twenty-Three

June 4, 1979

Dear Kimbra,

The worst thing about being put back in the hospital is realizing that I know too much. Last time I was ignorant—I had no grasp of what was happening to me. But this time, I do know. I know every test, every consequence of every test, every drug, every pain waiting for me. Sometimes, I get so depressed that I just want to give up.

Don't panic. I'm not giving up. Honest. There are two things keeping me going. Grandmother— who's practically driving Dr. Gallagher crazy with her suggestions—and Richard. He was so upset when he heard about my test results that he almost came right back home as soon as he got to Princeton. I begged him not to dump a whole year's worth of classwork for my sake. He has finals in a week and promises he'll remain and take

them. I'm glad. I don't want my illness to be a
burden on him.

It certainly doesn't look like I'll be going anywhere
anytime soon. My cancer is stubborn. Dr. Gallagher's throwing everything at it, but it just doesn't
want to take a hike. My head hurts so bad after
the spinal injections that I'm practically blind
from the pain.

But enough about my fun times. . . . How're you?
Please don't stop writing. The letters from you and
Elaine mean everything.

Love,
Jenny

July 10, 1979
Dear Jenny,

Mom forwarded your last letter to me at basketball
camp. I can't believe you've got to go through this a
second time—and you've got to go through it all by
yourself too! I swear, if I wasn't here at camp, I'd fly
down and move into your grandmother's and come
visit you every day.

Things are pretty good for me. The one arm isn't the
handicap the coaches thought it would be. I've
learned how to shield with my body and duck under
the person guarding me and dunk from the outside.
It's a pretty good maneuver, and believe it or not,
I've been a high scorer.

Don't get too discouraged. I know how much you
wanted to go out to your summer place, but it's only
July. You can go into remission and make it out there
yet. Just think. If the seas are choppy, you won't get
seasick, because your stomach is so used to upheaval!

Love,
Kimbra

July 25, 1979
Dear Jenny,
Cancer camp is a whole lot more fun than I ever thought it would be. I've met a bunch of girls, and I actually like a few of them. Not to worry. No one can ever take the place of you and Kimbra. We're the Three Musketeers, aren't we?
I met a cut guy here too. His name is Tony, and he had a brain tumor removed when he was twelve. He's doing fine now and has been coming to this camp for three years. He took me on a moonlight canoe ride, and it was positively magnifico. (Tony's teaching me Spanish. If fact, he's teaching me plenty of other things too.) If the three of us get together at Christmas like we're planning, I'll tell you and Kimbra all about it. Maybe.
Did I tell you that I've been recommended for my school's gifted program? What a joke! Me, gifted. Maybe it was all those chemo treatments. I don't know if I want to be gifted or not. Being smart is such a social downer in my school. Oh well . . . what's a person to do?

> *Love,*
> *Elaine*

August 5, 1979
Dear Elaine,
I'm jealous. Canoe rides in the moonlight sure beats elevator rides down to chemo. I've lost all my hair again. Somehow, it's not as important to me this time as it was last. All I want to do is get out of this place.
Richard's working at his dad's law firm again, and he comes by every day to visit. I can't believe I was such a dope about keeping him away last summer.

I mean, he doesn't care how I look (which is pretty awful). And it's so wonderful to have him around. Grandmother's a little jealous, I think, but she's tolerating it.

By the way, congrats on your gifted status. Noreen would have loved to blab it all around. Don't be afraid of being a "brain." Think of all the college offers you'll get. Brains are worth scholarship bucks, according to Richard.

Love,
Jenny

August 17, 1979
Dear Jenny,

Mom took me out to buy school supplies today. How do you like my purple ink? I'm actually looking forward to my junior year. I learned so much at basketball camp, and my high school coach is talking about my starting in January. I really think we have a shot at the state title this year.

Keep the faith! I worry about you.

Kimbra

August 26, 1979
Dear Kimbra,

I never thought I'd be jealous about someone returning to school, but I am. This was supposed to be the September I went back, but it looks like I'll be tutored again.

The good news is that I'm going home! Dr. Gallagher doesn't say much except that he wants me to get lots of rest and be comfortable. I have so many pills to take that Grandmother's hired Mrs. Kelly to live in and watch over my medications.

The one thing I'm looking forward to is Labor Day

weekend on Martha's Vineyard. Grandmother's flying us over even though the season is all but officially over. So what? Fewer tourists to bump into. Richard's coming too, and we'll finally get in a sail and a picnic. Can you believe we've been talking about doing this for a whole year?

I only wish I felt better. I'm tired, Kimbra. Tired of being sick, tired of taking treatments. Sometimes I wonder if I'll ever get well. Dr. Gallagher talks about new treatments coming along all the time, but some of them are a long way off. Right now, I'm simply trying to make it to 1980. Don't worry so much about me. I'm doing the best I can. Having Richard around helps, but I wish I could see you and Elaine too.

Love,
Jenny

PS. Elaine says she's got some flu bug, so she won't be returning to school on time either.

September 1, 1979
Dear Jenny,
Hope you and the hunk have the time of your lives. Have you ever thought of tying him to the mast of that sailboat and making him your love slave? It was just a thought.
Have fun, and then write and tell me all about it. And I want details!

Love,
Kimbra

Twenty-Four

THIS MUST BE *what heaven's like*, Jenny thought. She sat on the bow of Richard's boat and watched the hull slice through the water of the cobalt blue Atlantic. Behind her, Richard stood at the helm, and the magnificent white sail flapped in the stiff northerly breeze. Sun sparkled on the water like silver sequins; puffy clouds, chased by the wind, skidded across the blue sky; and tangy salt spray moistened her skin and stung her eyes. Yes . . . this was purely heaven.

Jenny wrapped her arms around her knees and pulled them against her chest. She wanted the brisk wind to blow away the smell of the hospital that clung to her skin. She wanted the sun to evaporate the stench of medications and treatments, of sickness and pain. Even though she wore a cable knit wool sweater and an oversize windbreaker, she was cold. But the scent of the sea was so delicious, the feel of the spray so luxurious, she couldn't bring herself to climb off the bow and return to the boat's cockpit, where she would be partially shielded.

"Ahoy! You all right?" Richard shouted, breaking the spell of sun and sea.

She turned and yelled, "I'm perfect."

"Why don't you come here and hold the helm for a spell?"

She knew he was trying to protect her. Her grandmother hadn't liked the idea of their going sailing at all. "It's too taxing," Marian had argued the night before. "Too much exertion for you."

"I'll be sitting down the whole time," Jenny insisted. "Richard will be doing all the work."

Marian had cast Richard a hard glance. "I won't do anything to hurt Jenny," Richard had contended.

"Don't forget to take your medicine on time," her grandmother called out as they'd left that morning.

How could she forget? Jenny wondered. She longed to throw the pills into the sea. They made her groggy and disoriented, but they did help check the constant pain she seemed to be in these days. The last time she'd been released from the hospital, she'd been weak, but at least she'd felt better than she did this time.

Richard studied Jenny as she sat curled up on the bow. She looked fragile to him, like a rose battered by wind and pelted by rain. She was impossibly thin. Her clothing hung on her frame. Dark circles rimmed her eyes, and her facial bones protruded from beneath pale, stretched skin.

He wanted to protect her, take care if her. If only he could. After he'd worked months to make Jenny let him into her life, Marian was trying to push him out. He felt a deep, growing resentment toward Jenny's grandmother. He and Marian had had an argument the night before, when Jenny had gone up to bed and he was preparing to leave.

Marian had ushered him to the front door of her summer home, where she had attempted to talk him out of their plan to go sailing and picnicking. "It's simply too long a day for her," Marian had stated. "She'll be totally worn out."

"She wants this, and I'm going to give it to her. I'll be careful. I'm not stupid, you know."

"That isn't the point."

"What is the point, Mrs. Crawford? Why are you working so hard to keep Jenny and me apart? Now that she's in remission again, I'd think you'd be doing everything to encourage her to get on with her life. I know I'm not the kind of man you want for Jenny, but I love her. And I'm not going to disappear now that she's on the mend. I don't care how many relapses she has, I'll be here for her."

Marian had pressed her lips together, refusing to comment. Finally, she'd given him a penetrating look and said, "Very well. Take her out tomorrow. Give her the good time she wants so much."

Marian's attitude had irked him. As if he were going to show her a bad time—

"What are you thinking about so hard?"

Jenny's question jerked Richard out of his thoughts. She had crawled back from the bow and was gazing at him through the ship's wheel. He grinned, hooked his elbow through the wheel to hold it steady, and helped her down. "I was thinking what a terrific-looking figurehead you make."

She jutted her upper body forward. "Like the ones sailors used to carve on the prows of old ships? Thanks. I love being called a relic."

Richard laughed heartily. "You're hardly a relic, Jennifer Warren Crawford."

"I don't know. . . . I think my bones are creaking."

"That's the ship's deck. Or maybe my stomach. What do you say I lower our mainsail and toss out the anchor, and we eat the grub your grandmother's cook packed for us?"

She wasn't hungry. She never had much of an appetite these days, but she agreed. He spread a blanket on the deck, padding it with cushions and life jackets from the quarters below deck. She helped him set the food out—enough to feed four people—and watched as he ate heartily.

"Peel you a grape?" he asked when he saw that she wasn't eating much.

"Aren't you kind. No . . . I'm enjoying watching you eat."

"You mean pig out, don't you?" She giggled, and he pulled her down so that her head rested in his lap. "Open wide."

She obeyed, and he placed a plump purple grape in her mouth. It tasted sweet and cool. "Very good," she said.

He stroked her cheek with the back of his hand. "Yes, very good."

His eyes glowed green as emeralds, and she felt the old, familiar yearning for him. "Why are you so nice to me?"

"Figure it out for yourself."

She tried to concentrate, to work out his enigmatic answer, but the gentle swell of the water beneath the boat, the warmth of the sun, and the sound of the lax sail fluttering overhead were making her eyelids grow heavy. "I'll have to figure it out later. Now I need to take a little nap." She hated losing even a minute of this wonderful day.

"A nap sounds good to me too." He stretched out alongside her, raised himself on one elbow, and gazed down on her upturned face.

"Just a little nap, all right? Wake me soon," she asked as her eyes closed.

He watched as she drifted off to sleep, and when he was certain that she slept, he bent and kissed each eyelid more softly than the summer breeze.

"But I want to go to the cave. You promised." Jenny jutted her lower lip stubbornly and refused to budge from the end of the dock.

"Jen, it's almost four o'clock. I'll bet your grandmother's pacing the floor looking for us." Richard tried to reason with her. They'd hit a headwind, and it had taken him far longer to bring the *Triple H* into port than he'd anticipated.

"I don't care. This is my special day, remember? I get to do whatever I want, and now I want to go to the cave."

There would be no reasoning with her, he knew. Even though he could see she was in pain, even though she refused to take one of her pain pills, she wasn't going to back down. "At least, let me call Marian," he said.

"No way. She'll pitch a fit and insist we come straight home. If we hurry, we can get to the cave and still be home before dark."

"It doesn't get dark until almost ten o'clock." He groaned. "She'll have my head."

"Since when did my grandmother start scaring you? You used to poke fun at her and make me laugh and feel very guilty about it." She tried to cajole him into giving her her way.

Before she had the power to keep me out of your life, Richard almost told Jenny. "All right, we'll go, but when your grandmother flies out of the house and puts her hands around my throat, I expect you to come to my rescue."

She giggled, temporarily erasing the lines of pain from around her mouth. He knew then that he would do anything for her and suffer the consequences later.

Quickly, he drove along the beach road, to its end, where there was nothing but curving beachfront and high granite bluffs facing the sea.

"It's even more beautiful than I remember," Jenny said, getting out of the car.

He had parked as close to the cliffs as possible, but they still had a long walk, to be followed by a stiff climb. "Are you sure you're up to this?"

"I'm going," she insisted.

They walked along the water's edge until it became impossible to avoid the jutting stone and swirling water. "Tide's coming in," he said. "I hope we can find the entrance."

"We'll find it."

He helped her struggle up the first layer of rock and inch westward around the surface. "The entrance's not easy to find." He was talking half to himself. "I was a kid of ten when I first found it."

"And you showed it to me that first summer I came to live with my grandmother. I'll never forget all the picnics we've had here over the years."

He felt for a partially hidden crevice, and when his fingers hooked around it, he knew he'd found the opening. "Duck," he told her, pulling her tightly against his chest.

Huddled together, they walked hunched for twenty feet, then the confinement ended and they stepped inside a vast cave.

Twenty-Five

~∽~

INSIDE THE CAVE, stalactites hung like icicles from the ceiling and along the walls in a rigid fringe. The ceiling soared to a small opening that allowed light to enter, but because the light was so diffused, the cave became lit in an ethereal blue. The formations stood out in blue etched relief, like carvings on grotto walls.

Tears swam in Jenny's eyes. "It's like coming home," she whispered as scenes from her childhood bombarded her.

Richard felt he'd stayed away far too long. Yet, it hadn't seemed right to come here without her during his few visits to his parent's island cottage over the summer. "Are you warm enough?"

The cave was damp and chilly, and she was cold, but she couldn't force herself to leave so soon. She hugged her arms to herself and walked across the granite floor toward the formation that they had used as a tabletop when they'd been younger. "Remember the times I served us tea?" she asked, ignoring his question.

"We brought it in a thermos and poured it into your grandmother's best china cups."

"I sneaked them out of the house."

Richard grinned. "But we never so much as chipped one of them, did we?"

"Never." She peered around the tabletop plateau. Something was nagging at her memory, something concerning Richard from last summer. If only her brain weren't so numb with pain, she would be able to remember. . . .

"Hey, look." Richard pointed upward.

The hole emitting rays from a setting sun resembled a halo, and as the beams filtered downward, they changed from bright blue, to lavender blue, to midnight blue. She stood beneath the hole, and blue light spilled over her.

Richard felt his breath catch. She seemed to come from another universe, beautiful and full of light.

"Come stand with me."

He went to her, and without speaking, they slid into each other's arms. "It's like being in a cathedral," she whispered, looking up at him. "Like a holy place only for us."

He couldn't stop himself from kissing her long and deep.

For Jenny, in that instant, her girlhood fantasies turned into reality. Richard was holding her, kissing her. Her heart raced, and her bones turned liquid. How long had she wished for this moment? How long had she dreamed about it? If only the light were magic and could turn them both to stone, then throughout time, they would be together.

Richard broke the kiss. He knew he should apologize, but the words stuck in his throat. He wasn't sorry one bit. He stroked her face and said, "I love you, Jenny." Once the words were out, he couldn't take them back.

"I've loved you forever," she told him in return. "Don't you know that by now?"

He touched his forehead to hers, clasped his fingers behind the small of her back, closed his eyes, and took a long, shuddering breath. He was angry with himself for letting himself go, for following his desires instead of his logic. She was too young. He'd taken advantage of her.

"You don't believe me, do you?" Jenny broke away and stepped backward out of the light.

"It's not that . . ."

"You think I'm just a kid with a crush." He said nothing. "That might have been true a year ago, but it isn't now. Don't you understand? This past year, I've been to hell and back, Richard. I know what pain is like. I know what love is like. I've felt them both."

"Jenny, I—"

"Hear me out." She held up her hand. "I've shared things with my friends . . . feelings . . . dreams. We may never get to live them out. But it doesn't stop us from wanting all the things other people want. Kimbra wants two arms again. Elaine wants to be well. *I* want to be well. We all want somebody to love us."

He started to speak, but she silenced him again. "Not loved just by our families, but by someone special who sees us from the inside out. Who loves us even when we're bald and scabby and ugly."

She took a deep breath and continued. "Life played a mean trick on me when my parents died.

But it gave me Grandmother ... to sort of balance the scales, I guess. Life played an even worse trick on me when it gave me leukemia. So how is that supposed to balance out, Richard? What will tip the scales this time and make cancer less horrible?"

She shook her head, and he saw tears trembling on her lashes. She said, "I don't know. I keep asking God, but I still don't know. If ... if you really love me, it would be a start."

He could hear her breathing echoing off the walls of the cave. Time was standing still, waiting for him to catch up. "I really love you."

She broke into sobs and flung herself into his arms. He kissed her, and she kissed him back. They sank to their knees, clinging to one another, raining kisses on lips, cheeks, foreheads, throats. They were in the light once more and glowing with blue-white fire. "Say it again," she pleaded between kisses. "Tell me again."

"I love you."

"Forever?"

"Forever."

The sun had long since set when Richard took her back to her grandmother's. Jenny didn't care how angry Marian was going to be. Nothing mattered except what she'd experienced in Richard's arms inside the cave. He loved her. She loved him. Not even the throbbing pain of her body could rob her of her joy.

"You're very late." Marian held open the door for them, but her steely gaze was only on Richard.

"It was my fault," Jenny said quickly. "I fell asleep out on the boat and Richard didn't have the heart to wake me. By the time I woke up, we had a headwind." It was a partial truth.

"You look blue from the cold."

Richard had driven home with the car heater on high, but still her teeth chattered. "I'll take a warm bath."

"I'm sorry, Mrs. Crawford," Richard said, hating not being able to tell her that he loved Jenny and wanted her with him. He didn't care whether Marian approved or not. Jenny *belonged* with him.

"I'll deal with you later." Marian's tone turned icy.

Anger flared, but Jenny squeezed his hand, and he swallowed his retort.

Marian took Jenny's free hand and rubbed it. Jenny wished it weren't so cold. "Your friend Kimbra's called three times," Grandmother said.

"Kimbra? What did she want?"

"She wouldn't tell me. She wants to talk to you."

"Maybe I'd better leave," Richard said.

"No!" Jenny hung on to his hand. She was suddenly frightened. Why would Kimbra have called— she knew that Jenny was supposed to call her Tuesday when she got back to Boston. "Stay with me until I talk to her."

Taken aback by the frightened look on her face, he agreed. He followed her into Marian's sun room and watched as her fingers fumbled with the ornate phone.

"Let me," her grandmother offered.

"I'll do it," Jenny insisted.

She listened as Kimbra's phone rang, her heart pounding. When Kimbra answered, Jenny asked lightly, "Checking up on me?"

"Oh, Jenny . . . Jenny, it's you." Kimbra's voice sounded choked.

"What's wrong?"

"Elaine's mother called this afternoon. Elaine's dead, Jenny. She's dead."

Jenny swayed, and Richard's arm shot around her. Words clogged her throat until she could barely whisper, "I don't believe it. How?" Her knuckles went white on the receiver. Marian started to take the phone away, but Richard's strong hand grasped her wrist. For a few moments, their gazes locked in silent battle, but it was Marian who backed off.

"Remember that flu she told us about? Well, she never got over it. She just got sicker and sicker. She went to the hospital, and they said her resistance was low because of all the chemo she's been taking."

"They didn't send her to Boston? To Dr. Gallagher?"

"She was too sick to move."

As Kimbra talked, Jenny began to feel disjointed, removed. A nonsensical nursery rhyme played over and over in her mind. *One little, two little, three little Indians* . . . "Jenny, Elaine's gone! Just like that."

Four little, five little, six little Indians . . . "I'll call her mother." Jenny said. "W-we'll do something . . ." *Six little, five little, four little Indians* . . . Jenny didn't remember what else she said to Kimbra, but eventually she hung up.

"Honey, what's the matter?" Grandmother asked.

"Two," Jenny said softly, holding up two fingers. "Only two little Indians left." Then she collapsed in Richard's arms.

Twenty-Six

Outside Jenny's bedroom window, the trees blazed with autumn colors. She was glad to be out of the hospital once more, but her days were dreadfully monotonous. It had been bad enough when she'd spent her birthday in the hospital in May, but now it looked as if she'd be spending her Christmas holiday in a room that was a replica of the hospital.

Bottles of pills lined her dresser. An oxygen tank stood beside her bed, next to an IV stand. Bedside tables, food trays, and strange equipment took up space in the room that had once sheltered dolls and teddy bears.

Grandmother had fixed up one of the guest rooms for Mrs. Kelly, who took care of Jenny full-time. The nurse changed IV bags twice a day, cleaned the catheter surgically implanted in Jenny's chest, doled out pills in prescribed order, and made certain that the linen was fresh and clean. Jenny drifted in and out of wakefulness, remembering her sailing trip with Richard, their time in the cave, the news about Elaine. . . .

Jenny had been too ill to attend the funeral, but Kimbra had gone and had written her all about it. Grandmother had promised to fly Kimbra in over Thanksgiving weekend, and that, coupled with Richard's coming for the holiday, was all that kept her going from day to day.

Richard . . . She turned her head, so that she could stare at his photograph. She missed him so much. But he was now in his junior year at Princeton, with definite plans to enter law school. His life was moving forward, while hers seemed on endless hold.

She'd had to give up her studies. "Time enough for that after Christmas," Grandmother had said when Jenny had cried over falling behind in her schoolwork. "Goodness, as bright as you are, you'll catch up and pass everyone else in no time."

Jenny appreciated all that her grandmother did for her. Every afternoon, Marian would bring her needlepoint into Jenny's room, where she worked even if Jenny slept. "I'm bad company," Jenny would say, if she dozed off.

"You're wonderful company. This is a special time for me. No phones . . . no interruptions. I get so much accomplished. And best of all, I get to be with you."

Jenny sometimes caught her grandmother staring at her sadly. She would see Marian's eyes mist over, then watch as she quickly dabbed away the moisture and proceed as if nothing had happened. Jenny hated knowing her illness caused her grandmother grief, but there was nothing she could do about it.

She did observe a difference in her routine from

previous at-home confinements. One day, she asked her grandmother about it. "How come I don't have to go in for outpatient treatments anymore?"

"Dr. Gallagher feels we can administer whatever you need right here," her grandmother explained.

"It seems strange. He's never done that before."

"You know doctors, just when you think you've got them figured out . . . Anyway, I thought you'd be glad not to go in. Don't tell me you want to."

"No way. I hope I never see the inside of that place again. Still, I think about the kids on the pediatric floor, and I miss them. I feel so sorry for the little ones because they don't understand why they're being tortured."

"Yes, it must seem like torture to them, but it's necessary. I know they must miss you. You were a help to them."

"Only a cure for cancer can help," Jenny insisted softly.

Now, Jenny's days seemed to melt into one another in an endless chain of pills and bed rest. She focused on the calendar next to Richard's picture. Another week until Thanksgiving. Then Christmas and a brand-new year. Perhaps things would turn around for her in 1980. She hoped so.

"Jenny's dying, isn't she?" With great effort, Richard kept his voice even. "I've been with her thirty minutes, and I can tell things are different this time. She's never going to get well, is she?"

He'd come home unexpectedly for the weekend, concerned about Jenny. It had been fun to surprise her, but her wasted appearance alarmed him, and so once she'd fallen asleep, he'd gone down to Marian to confront her. Marian studied him guardedly. "Be honest with me," he begged.

"All right," Marian said quietly. "The truth is, she'll never get well, but she doesn't realize it yet. Neither do I want her to."

Instantly, his stomach churned, and he had to clutch the edge of her desk for support. "Please tell me everything."

Marian pinched the bridge of her nose wearily. "The time between each relapse has been briefer, and each round of chemo more potent. Her last hospitalization was especially harrowing. I honestly didn't think I would even be able to bring her home."

He'd been away, and Jenny had almost died. The reality made cold fear sit like a stone in his stomach. Suddenly, he knew he'd done the right thing the night before, even though it had caused a heated argument with his father. Now, he had to tell Marian. But before dropping his bombshell, he asked, "Dr. Gallagher's giving up?"

"Dr. Gallagher's out of options." Marian resettled her glasses. "He says all we can do now is bring her home, make her comfortable, and . . . wait."

"How long?"

"Maybe another month."

Her words felt like blows to his midsection. "She kept talking about the new year and plans for school—"

"Pain control is our objective now. Mrs. Kelly is authorized to give her as much morphine as necessary so that she won't hurt."

A film of tears sprang up in Marian's eyes that she didn't bother to hide. Richard felt sorry for her. She was losing the one thing she loved above all else.

But, then, so was he. "I've dropped out of Princeton," he told her.

His announcement caused Marian to straighten in her chair. "You've what?"

"I think about Jenny all the time. I can't study. I can't concentrate in class. There's no sense in my staying there when I want to be here."

"I'm sure your father disagreed with your decision."

"He did at first. But I explained that I'll have the rest of my life to get my diploma and go to law school. I have only *now* with Jenny."

He toyed with the old inkwell on her desk. "In a way, Jenny's responsible for my even having a future."

"How so?"

"If she hadn't been who she is, I would have never gotten it together with my father. I would have wasted years of my life. Jenny made me dream dreams. She made me want to be somebody." He couldn't confess that his goals included to one day marry Jenny. "Now that I know time's running out for her . . ." He couldn't finish his sentence.

"Have you told Jenny about your decision?"

"Not yet."

"She'll suspect something's wrong. I—I don't want her knowing—"

"You can't stop her from knowing."

"But I *will* postpone it for as long as possible." Marian's eyebrow arched, and her tone was adamant.

"You should let her talk about dying. She needs to talk to someone about it." He wasn't sure how he knew that, but he did.

Marian stared at him for a long time, so long that

he began to grow nervous. Had he overstepped his bounds again? So what if he had! He couldn't stand on ceremonies now that he knew Jenny's days were numbered.

"You are not the man I would have wanted for her," Marian said.

"I know."

"But you've always been the one she's wanted for herself."

Her candor caught him by surprise. "I've loved her for a long time. I still love her, and I want to be with her. Not because she needs me, but because I need her." A hard knot formed in his throat.

Marian struggled slowly to her feet. She looked old to him and battle-weary. "I won't stand in your way, Richard. Her happiness is everything to me. It's all I have left to give her."

For an instant, he wanted to reach out and touch Marian Crawford. They were two people who loved the same person, who were going to lose the same person. Jenny had bound them together in an intricate and extraordinary way. He wasn't sure what future course that bonding would take. "Thank you," Richard said.

"We're setting up her special Christmas tree tonight. Perhaps you could carry her down to the sofa and let her tell you how she wants it decorated."

"I'd like that very much."

Marian walked to the door and paused. "I'll arrange for you to have a key to my house. That way, you can come and go as you like."

He was stunned. "I—I don't know what to say—"

"Make her happy. Make my Jenny happy for whatever time she has left."

Twenty-Seven

JENNY WAS SITTING in her bed and writing in a spiral notebook when her grandmother came into her room one December afternoon. "Richard said you wanted to see me."

Jenny lowered the notebook and smiled. The effort hurt, but she'd purposely told Mrs. Kelly to delay her routine dose of pain medication. She wanted a clear head when she talked to her grandmother. She had much to say and didn't want drugs to muddy her thought processes. "Come sit with me." Jenny patted the side of her bed.

Her grandmother complied. "I was coming later for my needlepoint session."

"I know, but I wanted to talk to you now."

"Is something the matter?"

"You mean besides never getting out of this bed?"

"Foolish question."

A pain seized Jenny, and she held her breath and wadded the sheets in her fists until it passed. She wiped a film of perspiration off her face and forced her thoughts back on course. "First of all, thank you for allowing Richard to hang around so much. It means so much to me to have him nearby."

"You mean a great deal to one another. It would be terrible of me to try and keep you apart."

"I don't know what the next few weeks will bring," Jenny began haltingly. "I know I'm fighting hard."

"Yes, you are."

"Don't look so sad. I'm going to be all right." She longed to give her grandmother some sense of peace about what was happening, but didn't know how. Jenny cleared her throat. "Actually, I need your help."

"My help? For what? Name it."

"I want you to help me make out my will." Her grandmother looked stricken, as if Jenny had suddenly let loose with an obscenity. Jenny hurriedly continued. "It's something I've wanted to do for a while, but I can't do it without you. You see, I learned some things when I spent so much time in the hospital. I learned that suffering does not respect people and who they are."

"That's very true."

"I know you understand because you lost Grandfather and then my dad." Marian nodded. "When I learned I had cancer, I was pretty scared. And no matter how many people were around me, I still felt alone. Things improved when I met others who were sick like me."

"You did seem happier once you made friends."

"They made a big difference, even though the worst part has been watching them die. Kimbra and I are the only ones left, and I'm not sure about myself." Jenny smiled at her own black humor. "I used to think about what I would do, what I'd be when I grew up. Mostly, I'd pick stupid things, like being a famous actress or a brilliant surgeon."

"You could be anything you wanted."

"Except healthy," Jenny said. "I can't be healthy."

"Please, dear, don't think negatively."

Jenny ignored her grandmother's well-intentioned comment and added, "So, I got to thinking about why God even bothered to put me on earth in the first place."

"For my sake, for Richard's . . . Your parents loved you very much."

"But is that enough? Why be put in people's life when you'll eventually bring them unhappiness when you go out of it?"

"You've enriched my life, Jenny. You've changed it forever."

"I couldn't go with my parents when they died. You can't come with me when I die."

"We'll all die someday, but then we'll be together again."

"I know that. But just because we can't take anything or anyone with us when we die, it doesn't mean we can't leave something meaningful behind."

"So that's why you want to write your will?"

"I'm very rich, aren't I?" Jenny answered her grandmother's question with a question of her own.

"You know you have a significant trust fund set up in your name."

Jenny nodded purposefully. "I want you to read something I've been working on for the past few days." She opened the spiral notebook, extracted a single sheet of paper, and watched her grandmother's face as she read silently. Naturally, she knew the contents by heart.

> Dear (insert selected person's name here),
>   You don't know me, but I know about you and because I do, I want to give you a special gift. Accompanying this letter is a certified check, my gift to you with no strings attached, to spend on anything you want. No one knows about this gift except you, and you are free to tell anyone you want.
>   Who I am isn't really important, only that you and I have much in common. Through no fault of our own, we have endured pain and isolation and have spent many days in a hospital feeling lonely and scared. I hoped for a miracle, but most of all I hoped for someone to truly understand what I was going through.
>   I can't make you live longer. I can't stop you from hurting, but I can give you one wish, as someone did for me. My wish helped me find purpose, faith, and courage.
>   Friendship reaches beyond time, and the true miracle is in giving, not receiving. Use my gift to fulfill your wish.
>
>   Your Forever Friend,
>   JWC

Her grandmother looked puzzled when she finished reading the letter Jenny had so carefully composed. "I'm not sure I understand," she said.

"I want to leave something meaningful behind. A special trust fund for other sick teenagers."

"For kids you've met at the hospital?"

"No. For complete strangers. And not just kids

who have cancer, but any kids who are terminally ill, with only a short time to live."

"But why strangers?"

"Why not strangers? Once I'm gone, everybody will be a stranger."

"Well, what's this about a wish that someone gave to you. What wish was that?"

"This one, of course. That you help set up this fund for me. I want to call it One Last Wish, and I want you to handle all the details.

Her grandmother's mouth dropped open. "You can't be serious."

"I haven't got time not to be serious." Jenny covered her grandmother's hands with hers. "You've always said you would do anything for me."

"Yes, but—"

"Well, this is what I want you to do. This is what I want to leave behind. I know Richard's father will help you if you ask. And I know you can make it work."

"But you haven't even signed your name to this letter. How will a recipient know where the money has come from?"

"I don't want anyone to know. Not ever. That's the other part of my wish—absolute secrecy. What good is a good deed if it isn't done in secret? No one can ever know. You and Mr. Holloway can figure out how to keep it a secret."

Marian sat speechless while Jenny watched a dozen emotions cross her face. "I'm not crazy, Grandmother. I know what I'm asking. I know it won't be easy, but I trust you to make it all happen. To make my last wish come true."

"And this certified check you speak of—did you have an amount in mind?"

Jenny took a deep breath. "I want to give each person one hundred thousand dollars. This money will be my legacy, as it was my father's and his father's before him. I mean, what good is money if you can't spend it? Or hope, if you can't pass it on?"

Twenty-Eight

❧

KNOWING THAT THE people she loved most in the world were close by gave Jenny a sense of well-being as the line between reality and unreality began to blur.

One afternoon, she woke from a deep sleep to see Kimbra sitting beside her bed, reading a magazine. "Is that you?" she asked. "Didn't you come at Thanksgiving?"

"Yes, but now I'm back." Kimbra smiled, dropped the magazine, and leaned toward Jenny. "It's almost time for Christmas. Your grandmother called the other night and said you were asking for me, so she arranged for me to fly down for the weekend."

"That's nice. I was wishing I could see you one more time."

"What's this 'one more time'? Don't you know you can't get rid of me?"

Jenny tried to smile, but she felt tired, so tired. "You look good. What is that you're wearing?"

"It's my letter jacket for basketball. Do you like it?" Kimbra stood and twirled so that Jenny could see the navy-and-gold jacket.

"I like it."

Kimbra sat back down. "I miss your letters to me."

"I want to write, but it's hard for me to hold a pen. And my handwriting's scribbly-looking."

"I know what you mean. I had to learn to write left-handed after I lost my arm. It took me ages to make my writing look legible."

Jenny reached out and touched Kimbra's empty sleeve. "I can't imagine you any other way. And someday, someone's going to like you exactly the way you are."

"Not any high school guys. They like the girls with no defects."

"Then you'll find someone in college. I know there's someone special waiting just for you."

Kimbra clasped Jenny's hand. "Well, I hope some guy likes me even half as much as Richard likes you. You're lucky. The two of you are a perfect match."

"I've loved him for years, and now that I know he really loves me back . . ." She let the sentence trail, and in the silence of the room, the ticking of the bedside clock could be heard. To Jenny, it sounded impatient, as if time wanted her to follow it to some distant universe where both could rest forever. "You're my best friend, Kimbra." She clung to her friend's hand, unwilling to let go of time and place.

"And you're my best friend, Jenny." Kimbra's voice began to quiver. "You're not going to do anything dumb, are you?"

"Like what?"

"Like . . . like what Elaine and Noreen did. I don't want to be the Lone Musketeer."

"I can't promise." Jenny watched a tear slide down Kimbra's cheek. "Don't cry. You're the tough one, remember?"

"Not tough enough. I'll never be tough enough."

Jenny hugged her with all the strength she had. "Why don't you read to me before you go? You know, like old times."

"I don't know if I can. . . ." Kimbra's voice was choked.

"Then just sit and hold my hand. And would you move that silly clock? It sounds like thunder, and it's giving me a headache."

When the weekend was over, and Kimbra had gone, Jenny told her grandmother, "Please take care of my friend. If she doesn't get a sports scholarship to college, make sure she has the money to go anyway. Will you do that for me?"

"If it's what you want."

"It's what I want."

Richard watched helplessly as Jenny went steadily downhill. Mrs. Kelly started her on oxygen round the clock two days after Christmas. Fluid kept building in Jenny's lungs, and Mrs. Kelly removed it with a syringe. The process was arduous and painful, but at least Jenny could breathe easier afterward.

Jenny grew obsessed with seeing the new year arrive, so her grandmother allowed her to keep the TV on at all times. It comforted Jenny to glance at it, to hear of the world's hopes and plans for the brand-new year.

Richard or her grandmother stayed with Jenny constantly. Richard found himself torn between wanting her alive and wanting her suffering to end.

Still, the thought of facing a lifetime without her was more than he could stand.

There were a thousand things he'd longed to tell her. Why had he waited so long? What had he been afraid of?

On New Year's Eve, Jenny slipped into a coma. Mrs. Kelly listened to her fluttering heartbeat and shook her head. "Hours, at the most," she told Richard and Marian.

"My poor baby." Her grandmother sat on the opposite side of Jenny's bed weeping, holding Jenny's hand and pressing it to her wet cheek.

"You can make it, Jenny," Richard whispered in her ear, for Mrs. Kelly had told him that hearing was the last sense a person kept. "Hang on, honey. I know you can make it."

In response, Jenny's chest heaved, and he was certain her hand moved in his.

On the TV, Richard, Marian, and Mrs. Kelly saw crowds gathering in Times Square. Jenny's room was cast in an eerie bluish light from the screen. Flakes of snow were falling outside her window. "Here it goes!" the TV announcer shouted, pointing to the ball that would drop down a pole to bring in the New Year.

A camera aimed at the ball of glowing light and showed it slowly descending as the crowd began to count down in unison. Richard watched Jenny's chest heave. "Almost," he whispered.

The crowd chanted, "Ten, nine, eight, seven . . ."

Richard squeezed Jenny's hand hard, hoping that the pressure would keep her linked to the real world. He felt desperate and determined to grant her her last wish—living to see 1980.

". . . six, five, four, three . . ."

He willed her chest to rise once more and fill with life-giving oxygen.

". . . two, one! Happy New Year!"

The crowd in Times Square erupted into one jubilant shout. Noisemakers and car horns sounded, firecrackers went off, and music began to play. "You made it, Jenny," Richard whispered in her ear. Time seemed slow but only seconds had passed. Jenny's chest stopped heaving. Suddenly her grip on Richard's hand went limp and motionless. Richard felt numbness steal over him. He watched as Mrs. Kelly placed a stethoscope over Jenny's heart. "She's left us," Mrs. Kelly whispered.

In the background, from the TV, Richard heard revelers singing, " 'Should auld acquaintance be forgot, And never brought to mind . . .' "

Richard climbed slowly along the rugged granite surface of the towering rocks, feeling for the crevice that would lead him to the entrance of the cave. *How many years has it been?* The last time he'd come to this spot, Jenny had been with him. *Beloved Jenny.*

His meeting with Marian hours before had brought back a rush of memories.

Marian had received him from her sickbed, tucked beneath a comforter, looking frail and old. "We must discuss the One Last Wish Foundation and then a project of my own," Marian had told him in a thin voice once he'd taken a chair beside her bed.

Through the years, his father had handled One Last Wish, investing Jenny's inheritance shrewdly through the economic boom years of the 1980s. The foundation was worth millions, and all the money was being given to ill teenagers, just as Jenny had requested.

"Jenny would be pleased to know how well the foundation's doing," Richard said. He looked across the room and saw that the portrait of Jenny painted years before was now hanging where Marian could see it from her bed.

"I had it shipped over from the house in Boston this summer," Marian explained. "She looks real enough to step off the canvas, doesn't she?"

"Yes," he whispered, unprepared for the bombardment of emotions churning through him.

"I miss her."

"I miss her too."

"Pity you've never married," Marian said quietly.

"I've never found the right woman. And now I'm pretty set in my ways. Besides, I'm busy running the firm." Richard shrugged and forced his eyes away from the portrait. "How can I help you, Marian? Tell me about this project you mentioned."

She shuffled through a sheaf of papers and handed them to him. "These explain everything in detail, but roughly, I'm in the process of establishing a retreat for young people like Jenny."

"A retreat?"

"A camp, a resort where very sick kids can come via special invitation. There, they can meet one another and simply enjoy the company of others like themselves. I've never forgotten how important it was to Jenny to be with others who were ill, as she was.

"I bought the property years ago, and over the past few years have had a complex built as fine as any luxury hotel. There are stables, pools, lakes for boating, and special medical facilities on the site. It's to be a place of rest and recreation where these young people can stay—perhaps live for a while and enjoy themselves."

He'd known that his father had been working on a project for Marian before his death, but had no idea this was it. "How can I help?" Richard asked. "Do you need me to go over the paperwork?"

Marian reached out and covered Richard's hand with hers. "Richard, I need you to run Jenny House . . . That's what I'm calling it." I need you to oversee its administration. To staff it, direct it, bring in kids to enjoy it. To see that its daily operation runs smoothly."

"I'm an attorney. Surely there are others—"

"You are the only person who loved Jenny as I did. The only one possible to implement this project. One Last Wish is Jenny's legacy. Jenny House is mine." Marian told him to think it over, but not to linger over his answer.

Once he'd left her, he'd come to the beach, hoping to figure out some kind of compromise. Managing such a place was out of his expertise. He wasn't qualified. He couldn't possibly do it.

His walk along the deserted beach had done nothing but add to his turmoil. Richard's fingers found the well-worn crevice in the rocky face of the cliff. He crouched and ducked inside, and when he straightened, he stood alone beneath the magnificent vaulted ceiling. Blue light spilled through the tiny opening high above. It seemed just as he and Jenny had left it years before.

He felt a knot wedge in his throat as he remembered kneeling with her on the stone floor and kissing her, holding her, loving her. If only she could be with him now. Hadn't he done everything possible to hold on to her?

"Why did you die, Jenny?" He gazed around the cave, along the cool, hard floor. He was alone. So alone.

Something glinted in the weak light, catching his eye. Richard walked toward the faint shimmer, stooped, and picked up the tattered remains of what had once been a picnic basket. Inside lay what was left of a velvet jewelry box. Time and salt corrosion and crabs had left the box in shreds.

He pulled away the remnants of the box and stared down—inside was a solid gold ID bracelet. He held it up. On one side was engraved: *Richard.* On the other: *With Love, Jenny.* He felt as if he'd had the wind knocked out of him.

Jenny had brought it to the cave years before, it had to be so. Why hadn't she given it to him? He'd never know, but he'd discovered this golden treasure and it was his—rightfully so. A gift from Jenny.

He put the bracelet around his wrist and shut the clasp. For a moment, Jenny's presence seemed so real that he thought she might suddenly appear, laughing, from behind the rocks. *Jenny Crawford, One Last Wish, Jenny House* . . . He belonged to all of them. He had his answer for Marian.

Richard hurried toward the cave's entrance, and rushed out of the darkness and into the brilliance of the sun.

Dear Reader,

For those of you who have been longtime readers, I hope you have enjoyed this One Last Wish volume. For those of you discovering One Last Wish for the first time, I hope you will want to read the other books that are listed in detail in the next few pages. From Lacey to Katie to Morgan and the rest, you'll discover the lives of the characters I hope you've come to care about just as I have.

Since the series began, I have received numerous letters from teens wishing to volunteer at Jenny House. That is not possible because Jenny House exists only in my imagination, but there are many fine organizations and camps for sick kids that would welcome volunteers. If you are interested in becoming such a volunteer, contact your local hospitals about their volunteer programs or try calling service organizations in your area to find out how you can help. Your own school might have a list of community service programs.

Extending yourself is one of the best ways of expanding your world . . . and of enlarging your heart. Turning good intentions into actions is consistently one of the most rewarding experiences in life. My wish is that the ideals of Jenny House will be carried on by you, my reader. I hope that now that we share the Jenny House attitude, you will believe as I do that the end is often only the beginning.

Thank you for caring.

YOU'LL WANT TO READ ALL THE ONE LAST WISH
BOOKS BY BESTSELLING AUTHOR

$\mathcal{I}$F YOU WANT TO KNOW MORE ABOUT MEGAN,

BE SURE TO READ

ON SALE NOW FROM BANTAM BOOKS
0-553-56067-0

Excerpt from *Let Him Live* by Lurlene McDaniel
Copyright © 1993 by Lurlene McDaniel

Published by Bantam Doubleday Dell Books for Young Readers
a division of Random House, Inc.
1540 Broadway, New York, New York 10036

$\mathcal{B}$eing a candy striper isn't Megan Charnell's idea of an exciting summer, but she volunteered and can't get out of it. Megan has her own problems to deal with. Still, when she meets Donovan Jacoby, she find herself getting involved in his life.

Donovan shares with Megan his secret: An anonymous benefactor has granted him one last wish, and he needs Megan's help. The money can't buy a compatible transplant, but it can allow Donovan to give his mother and little brother something he feels he owes them. Can Megan help make his dream come true?

"When I first got sick in high school, kids were pretty sympathetic, but the sicker I got and the more school I missed, the harder it was to keep up with the old crowd," Donovan explained. "Some of them tried to understand what I was going through, but unless you've been really sick . . ." He didn't finish the sentence.

"I've never been sick," Meg said, "but I really do know what you're talking about."

He tipped his head and looked into her eyes. "I believe you do."

$\mathcal{I}$F YOU WANT TO KNOW MORE ABOUT

KATIE AND JOSH, BE SURE TO READ

ON SALE NOW FROM BANTAM BOOKS
0-553-29842-9

Excerpt from *Someone Dies, Someone Lives* by Lurlene McDaniel
Copyright © 1992 by Lurlene McDaniel

Published by Bantam Doubleday Dell Books for Young Readers
a division of Random House, Inc.
1540 Broadway, New York, New York 10036

*K*atie O'Roark feels miserable, though she knows she's incredibly lucky to have received an anonymous gift of money. The money can't buy the new heart she needs or bring back her days as a track star.

A donor is found with a compatible heart, and Katie undergoes transplant surgery. While recuperating, she meets Josh Martel and senses an immediate connection. When Katie decides to start training to realize her dream of running again, Josh helps her meet the difficult challenge.

Will Katie find the strength physically and emotionally to live and become a winner again?

From the corner of her eye, Katie saw a boy with red hair who was about her age. He stood near the doorway, looking nervous. With a start, she realized he was watching her because he kept averting his gaze when she glanced his way. Odd, Katie told herself. Katie had a nagging sense she couldn't place him. As nonchalantly as possible, she rolled her wheelchair closer, picking up a magazine as she passed a table.

She flipped through the magazine, pretending to be interested, all the while glancing discreetly toward the boy. Even though he also picked up a magazine, Katie could tell that he was preoccupied with studying her. Suddenly, she grew self-conscious. Was something wrong with the way she looked? She'd thought she looked better than she had in months when she'd left her hospital room that afternoon. Why was he watching her?

Katie is also featured in the novels *Please Don't Die, She Died Too Young,* and *A Season for Goodbye.*

$\mathscr{I}$F YOU WANT TO KNOW MORE ABOUT SARAH,

BE SURE TO READ

ON SALE NOW FROM BANTAM BOOKS
0-553-29811-9

Excerpt from *Mother, Help Me Live* by Lurlene McDaniel
Copyright © 1992 by Lurlene McDaniel

Published by Bantam Doubleday Dell Books for Young Readers
a division of Random House, Inc.
1540 Broadway, New York, New York 10036

*S*arah McGreggor is distraught when she learns she will need a bone marrow transplant to live. And she is shocked to find out that her parents and siblings can't be donors because they aren't her blood relatives. Sarah never knew she was adopted.

As Sarah faces this devastating news, she is granted one last wish by an anonymous benefactor. With hope in her heart, she begins a search for her birth mother, who gave her up fifteen years ago. Sarah's life depends on her finding this woman. But what will Sarah discover about the true meaning of family?

Didn't the letter from JWC say she could spend it on anything she wanted? What could be more important than finding her birth mother? What could be more important than discovering if she had siblings with compatible bone marrow? Her very life could depend on finding these people. Sarah practically jumped up from the sofa. "I've got to go," she said.

𝒯F YOU WANT TO KNOW MORE ABOUT ERIC,

BE SURE TO READ

ON SALE NOW FROM BANTAM BOOKS
0-553-29809-7

Excerpt from *A Time to Die* by Lurlene McDaniel
Copyright © 1992 by Lurlene McDaniel

Published by Bantam Doubleday Dell Books for Young Readers
a division of Random House, Inc.
1540 Broadway, New York, New York 10036

$\int$ ixteen-year-old Kara Fischer has never considered herself lucky. She doesn't understand why she was born with cystic fibrosis. Despite her daily treatments, each day poses the threat of a lung infection that could put her in the hospital for weeks. But her close friendship with her fellow CF patient Vince and the new feelings she is quickly developing for Eric give her the hope to live one day at a time.

When an anonymous benefactor promises to grant a single wish with no strings attached, Kara finds a way to let the people who have loved and supported her throughout her illness know how much they mean to her. But will there be time for Kara to see her dying wish fulfilled?

"What am I going to do about you, Kara?"

Eric's tone was subdued and so sincere that his question caught her by surprise. "What do you mean?"

"I can't stay away from you."

"You seem to be doing a fine job of it," she said quietly, but without malice.

"I know it seems that way, but you don't know how hard it's been."

She was skeptical. "We just danced together, but after tonight, how will it be between us? Will you still ignore me in the halls? Will you duck into the nearest open door whenever you see me coming?"

He turned his head and she saw his jaw clench. She thought he might walk away, but instead he asked, "What's between you and Vince?"

$\mathcal{I}$F YOU WANT TO KNOW MORE ABOUT MORGAN,

BE SURE TO READ

ON SALE NOW FROM BANTAM BOOKS
0-553-29932-8

Excerpt from *Sixteen and Dying* by Lurlene McDaniel
Copyright © 1992 by Lurlene McDaniel

Published by Bantam Doubleday Dell Books for Young Readers
a division of Random House, Inc.
1540 Broadway, New York, New York 10036

*I*t's hard for Anne Wingate and her father to accept the doctors' diagnosis: Anne is HIV-positive. Seven years ago, before blood screening was required, Anne received a transfusion. It saved her life then, but now the harsh reality can't be changed—the blood was tainted. Anne must deal with the inevitable progression of her condition.

When an anonymous benefactor promises to grant Anne a single wish with no strings attached, she decides to spend the summer on a ranch out west. She wants to live as normally as she possibly can. The summer seems even better than she dreamed, especially after she meets Morgan. Anne doesn't confide in Morgan about her condition and doesn't plan to. Then her health begins to deteriorate and she returns home. Is there time for Anne and Morgan to meet again?

Fearfully, Anne stared at her bleeding hand.

Morgan reached beneath her, lifted her, and placed her safely away from the hay and its invisible weapon. "Let me see how bad you're cut."

"It's nothing," Anne said, keeping her hand close to her body. "I'm fine."

"You're not fine. You're bleeding. You may need stitches. Let me wipe it off and examine it."

Her eyes widened, reminding him of a deer trapped in headlights. "No! Don't touch it!"

"But—"

"Please—you don't understand. I—I can't explain. Just don't touch it." Wild-eyed, panicked, she spun, and clutching her hand to her side, she bolted from the barn.

Dumbfounded, Morgan watched her run back toward the cabin.

You MAY ALSO WANT TO READ

ON SALE NOW FROM BANTAM BOOKS
0-553-29810-0

Excerpt from *Mourning Song* by Lurlene McDaniel
Copyright © 1992 by Lurlene McDaniel

Published by Bantam Doubleday Dell Books for Young Readers
a division of Random House, Inc.
1540 Broadway, New York, New York 10036

*I*t's been months since Dani Vanoy's older sister, Cassie, was diagnosed as having a brain tumor. And now the treatments aren't helping. Dani is furious that she is powerless to help her sister. She can't even convince their mother to take the girls on the trip to Florida Cassie has always longed for.

Then Cassie receives an anonymous letter offering her a single wish. Dani knows she can never make Cassie well, but she is determined to see Cassie's dream come true, with or without their mother's approval.

Dani had rehearsed the speech so many times that even she was beginning to believe it. "It's as if you're supposed to do this. While we don't know who gave you the money for a wish, I think you should use it to get something you've always wanted. Listen, even a trillion dollars can't make you well, but the money you've gotten can help you have some fun. I say let's go for it! You deserve to see the ocean, whether Mom agrees or not. I'm going to help you make your wish come true."

$\mathcal{I}$F YOU WANT TO KNOW MORE ABOUT RICHARD
HOLLOWAY AND JENNY CRAWFORD,
BE SURE TO READ

ON SALE NOW FROM BANTAM BOOKS
0-553-56134-0

Excerpt from *The Legacy: Making Wishes Come True* by Lurlene McDaniel
Copyright © 1993 by Lurlene McDaniel

Published by Bantam Doubleday Dell Books for Young Readers
a division of Random House, Inc.
1540 Broadway, New York, New York 10036

*W*ho is JWC, and how was the One Last Wish Foundation created? Follow JWC's struggle for survival against impossible odds and the intertwining stories of love and friendship that developed into a legacy of giving. And discover the power that one individual's determination can have, in this extraordinary novel of hope.

"I had my physician call the ER doctor and afterward, when we discussed their conversation, he suggested that I get her to a specialist as quickly as possible."

"A specialist at Boston Children's," Richard said with a nod. "What kind of specialist?"

"A pediatric oncologist."

Before Richard could say another word, Jenny's grandmother spoke. "A cancer specialist," Marian said, her voice catching. "They believe Jenny has leukemia."

$\mathcal{I}$F YOU WANT TO KNOW MORE ABOUT KATIE,

CHELSEA, AND LACEY,

BE SURE TO READ

ON SALE NOW FROM BANTAM BOOKS
0-553-56262-2

Excerpt from *Please Don't Die* by Lurlene McDaniel
Copyright © 1993 by Lurlene McDaniel

Published by Bantam Doubleday Dell Books for Young Readers
a division of Random House, Inc.
1540 Broadway, New York, New York 10036

*W*hen Katie O'Roark receives an invitation from the One Last Wish Foundation to spend the summer at Jenny House, she eagerly says yes. Katie is ever grateful to JWC, the unknown person who gave her the gift that allowed her to receive a heart transplant. Now Katie is asked to be a "big sister" to others who, like her, face daunting medical problems: Amanda, a thirteen-year-old victim of leukemia; Chelsea, a fourteen-year-old candidate for a heart transplant; and Lacey, a sixteen-year-old diabetic who refuses to deal with her condition. As the summer progresses, the girls form close bonds and enjoy the chance to act "just like healthy kids." But when a crisis jeopardizes one girl's chance of fulfilling her dreams, they discover true friendship and its power to endure beyond this life.

"Me, too. I don't know what I'd do without you, Katie. Whenever I think about last summer, about how you were so close to dying . . ."

She didn't allow him to complete his sentence. "Every day is new, every morning, Josh. I'm glad I got a second chance at life. And after meeting the people here at Jenny House, after making friends with Amanda, Chelsea, and even Lacey, I want all of us to live forever."

He grinned. "Forever's a long time."

She returned his smile. "All right, then at least until we're all old and wrinkled."

*I*F YOU WANT TO KNOW MORE ABOUT
KATIE AND CHELSEA, BE SURE TO READ

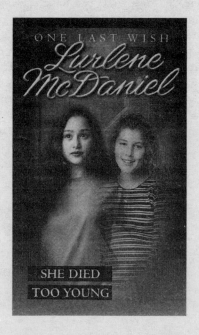

ON SALE NOW FROM BANTAM BOOKS
0-553-56263-0

Excerpt from *She Died Too Young* by Lurlene McDaniel
Copyright © 1994 by Lurlene McDaniel

Published by Bantam Doubleday Dell Books for Young Readers
a division of Random House, Inc.
1540 Broadway, New York, New York 10036

*C*helsea James and Katie O'Roark met at Jenny House and spent a wonderful summer together.

Now Chelsea and her mother are staying with Katie as Chelsea awaits news about a heart transplant. While waiting for a compatible donor, Chelsea meets Jillian, a kind, funny girl who's waiting for a heart-lung transplant. The two girls become fast friends. When Chelsea meets Jillian's brother, he awakens feelings in her she's never known before. But as her medical situation grows desperate, Chelsea finds herself in a contest for her life against her best friend. Is it fair that there's a chance for only one of them to survive?

"Don't you see? There's one donor coming in. Only one. Who will the doctors save? Who will get the transplant?"

For a moment Josh stared blankly as her question sank in. "Katie, you don't know for sure there's only one donor."

"Yes, I do. There's only one. One heart. Two lungs. The doctor said the donor's family had given permission for all her organs to be donated." Katie's voice had risen with the tide of panic rising in her. "There's two people in need and only one heart."

Katie and Chelsea are also featured in the novels *Please Don't Die* and *A Season for Goodbye*.

$\mathcal{I}$F YOU WANT TO KNOW MORE ABOUT LACEY,

BE SURE TO READ

ON SALE NOW FROM BANTAM BOOKS
0-553-56264-9

Excerpt from *All the Days of Her Life* by Lurlene McDaniel
Copyright © 1994 by Lurlene McDaniel

Published by Bantam Doubleday Dell Books for Young Readers
a division of Random House, Inc.
1540 Broadway, New York, New York 10036

*O*ut of control—that's how Lacey Duval feels in almost every aspect of her life. There's nothing she can do about her parents' divorce, there's nothing she can do about the death of her young friend, there's nothing she can do about having diabetes—that's what Lacey believes.

After a special summer at Jenny House, Lacey is determined to put her problems behind her. When she returns to high school, she is driven to become a part of the in crowd. But Lacey thinks fitting in means losing weight and hiding her diabetes. She starts skipping meals and experimenting with her medication—sometimes ignoring it altogether.

Her friends from the summer caution her to face her problems before catastrophe strikes. Is it too late to stop the destructive process Lacey has set in motion?

She went hot and cold all over. It was as if he'd shone a light into some secret part of her heart and something dark and ugly had crawled out. She had rejected Jeff because she didn't want a sick boyfriend. She'd said as much to Katie at Jenny House.

"It's any sickness, Jeff. It's mine too. I hate it all. I know it's not your fault, but it's not mine either."

"I'll bet no one at your school knows you're a diabetic."

She said nothing.

"I'm right, aren't I?"

"It's none of your business."

"You know, Lacey, you're the person who won't accept that you have a disease. Why is that?"

She whirled on him. "How can you ask me that when you've just admitted that girls drop you once they discover you're a bleeder? You of all people should understand why I keep my little secret."

Lacey is also featured in the novels *Please Don't Die* and *A Season for Goodbye*.

$\mathcal{I}$F YOU WANT TO KNOW MORE ABOUT KATIE,
CHELSEA, AND LACEY, BE SURE TO READ

ON SALE NOW FROM BANTAM BOOKS
0-553-56265-7

Excerpt from *A Season for Goodbye* by Lurlene McDaniel
Copyright © 1995 by Lurlene McDaniel

Published by Bantam Doubleday Dell Books for Young Readers
a division of Random House, Inc.
1540 Broadway, New York, New York 10036

*T*ogether again. It's been a year since Katie O'Roark, Chelsea James, and Lacey Duval shared a special summer at Jenny House. The girls have each spent the year struggling to fit into the world of the healthy. Now they're back, this time as "big sisters" to a new group of girls who also face life-threatening illnesses.

But even as the friends strive to help their "little sisters" face the future together, they must separately confront their own expectations. Katie must decide between an old flame and an exciting scholarship far from home. Chelsea must overcome her fear of romance. And Lacey must convince the boy she loves that her feelings for him can be trusted.

When tragedy strikes Jenny House, each of the girls knows that things can never be the same. Will Lacey, Chelsea, and Katie find a way to carry on the legacy of Jenny House? Can their special friendship endure?

"Over here!" Katie called. "I found it."

Chelsea and Lacey hurried to where Katie was crouched, digging through a pile of dead leaves. The tepee was partially buried, and Chelsea held her breath, hoping that the laminated photo and Jillian's diamond stud earring were still tied to it.

"It's come apart," Katie said, lifting up the twigs in three parts. But from the corner of one of the sticks, the laminated photo dangled, and from its center the diamond caught the afternoon sunlight.

The photo looked faded, but Amanda still smiled from the center of their group. Chelsea felt a lump form in her throat. These days, she and Katie and Lacey looked older, more mature, healthier too. But Amanda looked the same, her gamine smile frozen in time. And ageless.

Katie took the photo from Lacey's trembling fingers. "We were quite a bunch, weren't we?"

𝒴OU CAN READ MORE ABOUT
MANY OF YOUR FAVORITE CHARACTERS FROM
THE ONE LAST WISH BOOKS IN

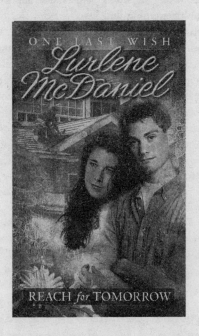

ON SALE NOW FROM BANTAM BOOKS
0-553-57109-5

Excerpt from *Reach for Tomorrow* by Lurlene McDaniel
Copyright © 1999 by Lurlene McDaniel

Published by Bantam Doubleday Dell Books for Young Readers
a division of Random House, Inc.
1540 Broadway, New York, New York 10036

*K*atie O'Roark is thrilled to learn that Jenny House is being rebuilt. After the fire last year, Katie thought she could never return to the camp, where she spent the summers with young men and women like her who faced medical odds that were stacked against them. But thanks to Richard Holloway's efforts, Katie and her longtime friends Lacey and Chelsea will work as counselors once again. They'll be joined by Megan Charnell, Morgan Lancaster, and Eric Lawrence, who are newcomers to Jenny House but who have experienced the generosity of the One Last Wish Foundation.

It's not until Katie arrives at camp that she discovers that Josh Martel, her former boyfriend, is also a counselor. Katie and Josh broke up a year ago, when Katie decided to go away to college. Being near Josh again brings back a flood of old emotions for Katie. And when Josh confronts unexpected adversity, Katie knows she has to work out her feelings for him. Through the heart transplant she underwent years ago, Katie miraculously received a gift of new life. Now she must discover how to make the most of that precious gift and choose her future.

She stopped. By now tears had filled her eyes and her heart felt as if it might break. She truly believed that God had heard her prayer. What she did not know was whether or not he would grant her request. Against great odds, God had given her a new heart when she'd desperately needed one. And he had brought Josh into her life as well. She believed that with all her heart and soul. Now there was nothing more she could do except wait. And have faith.

Katie lifted her arms in the moonlight in supplication to the heavens.